"Why haven't you ever gotten married?"

"I reckoned there was no way any woman could domesticate me into a housecat."

She shifted in his lap, and her hair tickled his chin. He glanced down and caught a faint smile tugging at her lips. "Some detective you are. You don't know anything about women, Joe Watchman."

"Hey, I'm a great detective! Everyone at that Detroit agency where I used to work said so. When another agent needed to track down a criminal, he'd ask me to put my ear to the pavement. Sure enough, I'd—"

"You're incorrigible!" She snuggled closer against him. "Come on, big shot, tell me more of your exploits."

He talked of a few. Invented others merely for her entertainment. At last she fell asleep, and he carried her to the bed. Then he returned to the den to pace.

His head was too full of her. He felt as if he might never sleep again.

Dear Reader:

In May of 1980 Silhouette had a goal. We wanted to bring you the best that romance had to offer—heartwarming, poignant stories that would move you time and time again.

Mission impossible? Not likely, because in 1980 and all the way through to today, we have authors with the same dream we have—writers who strive to bring you stories with a distinctive medley of charm, wit, and above all, *romance*.

And this fall we're celebrating in the Silhouette Romance line—we're having a Homecoming! In September some of your all-time favorite authors are returning to their "alma mater." Then, during October, we're honored to present authors whose books always capture the magic—some of the wonderful writers who have helped maintain the heartwarming quality the Silhouette Romance line is famous for.

Come home to Romance this fall and for always. Help celebrate the special world of Silhouette Romance.

I hope you enjoy this book and the many books to come.

Sincerely,

Tara Hughes
Senior Editor
Silhouette Books

PARRIS AFTON BONDS

Run to Me

Published by Silhouette Books New York

America's Publisher of Contemporary Romance

To Lana Wilkes: A lovely lady and a lovely human
being. I couldn't ask for a better sister-in-law.
And to Jackie: You are special to me because you are
a part of me, a part of what I was and what I am.

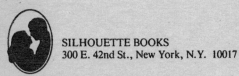

SILHOUETTE BOOKS
300 E. 42nd St., New York, N.Y. 10017

Copyright © 1987 by Parris Afton Bonds

ISBN: 0-373-08526-5

First Silhouette Books printing September 1987

All the characters in this book are fictitious. Any
resemblance to actual persons, living or dead, is
purely coincidental.

SILHOUETTE, SILHOUETTE ROMANCE and colophon
are registered trademarks of the publisher.

America's Publisher of Contemporary Romance

Printed in the U.S.A.

PARRIS AFTON BONDS

has been writing since she was six, though she didn't turn professional until her family moved to Mexico. She gives credit for her several literary awards to her husband and sons, who have given unstintingly of their love and support.

Chapter One

She was running. Running scared. Running out of money. Running out of gas.

Next she would run out of time.

How long could a healthy person survive in this desert without shelter or water? One day, wasn't it? Ten to twelve pounds of body fluid evaporated daily, if she remembered correctly from her childhood years on the high desert of eastern Arizona.

The desert was a labyrinth of arroyos and dunes, and she was hopelessly lost on a narrow blacktop road that meandered beneath the cloudless blue-hot sky. She had always been puzzled that the Hopi and

Navajo hadn't become lost tribes in this sun-bleached wasteland.

On either side of the road sheets of pockmarked lava sloped away in overlapping folds. Distant mesas sat like Indian women, the rocky brown palisades looking like flounced skirts. In between, nothing. Not a hogan or a shepherd. Only the dense shimmer of superheated air that gave the illusion of water rippling on the road. With the Lincoln's air conditioning switched off to conserve on gas and the electric windows down, the black tar of the road smelled rank in the hot August afternoon.

Then, rising out of the wavering air, she spotted a large, corrugated, shedlike building. Hanging from the building was a sign—an Indian profile with a corroded eye—that promised Red Man tobacco inside. Her heart leaped with hope. Human habitation. Outside the building, drums stenciled "Exxon" also held forth a promise. Gasoline!

She parked in front. With an anxious glance at the seven-year-old, asleep on the front seat beside her, she quietly got out, leaving the door open to allow the merest breath of stirring air to enter. Under the porch's slatted eaves a tin Pepsi sign sported a broken thermometer. The screen door, with holes in it as large as half dollars, swung creakily on its rusted hinges.

The store's interior was equally deteriorated. The gasket-rimmed lid of a peeling, cold drink cooler was open to reveal only emptiness. The glass top of a wall-long counter was cracked and chipped, and behind it the bare shelves were dusty. The store was a tombstone to past aspirations, its owner disillusioned and long gone.

The air inside the store was stale, and its dry, roasting heat fairly shriveled the flesh on her bones. With a grim sigh she pushed open the screen door and went back out to stand on the porch. The air outside was a little better. At two o'clock, the hottest time of the day, the shafts of sunlight slanted between the wooden beams the natives called *vigas* with a laser-hot intensity.

Reluctantly she stepped out into the fierce, color-killing sunlight. Feeling its rays blistering her scalp, she strode quickly to the gasoline drums, surrounded by weeds. One by one, she tried to pry off the lids. They wouldn't budge. Worse, when she rapped on the drums, the hollow sound gave her her answer: empty.

Absently, she wiped at the sweat that trickled along the vee opening of her raw-silk blouse, darkening its carnation color. Across the blacktop road, dust devils wove back and forth on the sun-struck desert. She swallowed hard, feeling fear beat at her with its batlike wings. She couldn't let him catch up with her. But he would. He had promised her that there was no place she could run where he wouldn't find her.

And she believed him.

But she would never surrender.

She hurried back to the car and gunned the engine, thoughtlessly consuming precious gas. She was on the run again. And this time she was running out of hope.

He crouched over her. The half-naked woman was the colors of the desert. White where the high noon sunlight fell, pale brown in the shadows cast by a perfectly shaped arm that was draped across her rib-cage, and deep blue on the under-slopes of her breasts.

Her features, taken separately, were not classically beautiful. Thick, black brows, only slightly arched, but adding drama to her face. Lips that were asymmetrically shaped and badly cracked from sunburn. Too full, though, to suggest any self-restraint. A high forehead. Her skin, hot and dry, was blistered, so it was difficult to judge its merits. A rather ordinary nose.

He looked for other things in faces, however. Intangible things. The striking individuality of her bone structure, he noted, indicated a combination of confidence and care. Altogether her face was a

pleasant one. No, more than that. A sensuous one.
Even with her blouse ridiculously turbaned about her
head. What color was her hair?

And what the hell was she doing in the middle of
twenty-five thousand square miles of Indian reservation wilderness? Besides dying from dehydration,
that was. The asphalt strip of New Mexico's Navajo
Route 9 was more than forty miles to the south.

Quickly his metallic gaze tracked the baked sand
around and beyond her, learning her story. Stretch-
ing behind her, to the north, were her footprints. He
glanced down at the object she was cradling in one
scratched and bloody palm. A pebble. Nearby lay a
strand of rusted wire, with a noose looped at one
end.

The abandoned trading post. The wire would have
come from the trading post some four miles back
along the road.

This mysterious woman must have had experience
in the desert. He could tell by the sweat-dampened
blouse tied about her head. The pebble to put in her
mouth and control thirst. The wire for catching liz-
ards, or maybe a tiger salamander, to eat raw for
moisture.

The gold nugget bracelet and Rolex watch, however, belied such a primitive life-style. It didn't seem
likely that she had ever scratched out an existence on
scrub land like this. Her kind mostly spoke two lan-

guages: English and Gucci. He aligned his fingers along the column of her neck, feeling its milky softness. Her pulse was thready. She was alive, but only barely.

He scooped her up easily against his chest and rose. The hot desert air tugged at the breech clout he had worn to the Wind Song Ceremony—the only thing he was wearing, if his knee-high moccasins and incongruous blue baseball cap were discounted. With her slung in the hammock created by his arms—she was as slight as a child—he half trotted back to the white carryall with its humped buffalo insignia of the Law and Order Division of the Bureau of Indian Affairs.

She moaned when he lowered her into the shade cast by the four-wheeler. Taking his clipboard off the dashboard, he entered the time and date and noted the unconscious woman's race and age, which he reckoned at about thirty. Then he signed his name.

So much for idiotic rules and regulations and his FBI Academy training.

The beer in his half-empty aluminum can was hot and stale, but its salt content would work wonders. He saved the cans for old Uncle Thin Man, who cut them up and put them over his corn shoots in the spring, and now he was glad not to have tossed this one away when the beer grew warm.

He hunkered over her again, his weight on the balls of his feet, and, supporting the back of her head with his hand, he held the can's rim to her mouth. "Just drink a little bit," he said when, her eyes still closed, she began to gulp the beer like a greedy nestling. "It's going to be all right."

She had amazing lashes. They swept downward, curling slightly with pliant silkiness. He wished she would open her eyes. He wanted to see what color they were. Blue? Dead eyes, he called them, because blue irises didn't have any pigment.

"It's going to be all right," he reassured her—and himself—again. "Right now, we just have to get your temperature down. You've got heat prostration."

Luckily she hadn't gotten more sunburned or she wouldn't have made it. Had there been anyone with her? "Drink a little bit more. Just sip it."

Her lids fluttered open. He found himself smiling. Gray green. Like desert vegetation—the juniper and cedar and spiny saguaro. And a mesmerizingly sensuous shape, with an otherworldly quality. Intelligence glowed in their depths.

"Danny," she whispered through parched lips.

Who was Danny?

"Save him. He's in the swimming pool... drowning. Save him!"

Delirious. Precious time could be wasted backtracking for her nonexistent Danny. But he'd risk it.

Not far. Maybe twenty miles. That was as far as she could possibly have walked in the space of a night, considering her condition.

He laid her in the back seat of the carryall, trying to ignore the invitation of her soft, feminine curves. His curiosity, however, got the better of him on one point. Gingerly, like an archeologist uncovering a four-thousand-year-old vase that could turn to dust in his hands, he unwrapped the blouse from her head. A quantity of satiny hair, the color of root-beer, spilled onto her shoulders and over the edge of the car seat. Silky strands curled willfully about his fingers. He felt an elaborate wave of delight. Gratified now, he shut the back door and turned the four-wheeler in the direction of the abandoned trading post.

Good thing he had had to check out the Wind Song Ceremony held back in Chee Canyon last night, or he would never have chanced across the unconscious woman. The ceremony required a strict degree of observance, uncontaminated by the white world and its trappings, such as clothing and food. But he had found Ted Chinle sitting in an alcoholic stupor in the middle of Navajo 9, wearing a toy gun belt with a bottle of Thunderbird wine stuffed in each holster. No doubt he had fallen off the back of a crowded pickup returning from the ceremony. Joe had loaded him in the carryall and returned him to his hogan.

And now here was another unconscious body. Must be his day for playing good Samaritan.

His constantly scanning gaze picked up an object—no, objects—ahead. Her purse and, a little farther on, a pair of shoes. He slowed down and leaned out the open door to scoop them up. They were of black alligator, and the shoes had spiked heels. So this lady didn't wear sneakers. She would probably crawl first.

A mile from the trading post he spotted the car: a long black Lincoln, doors flung wide. It had to be hotter than an oven inside. At least it offered shade to anyone who might be inside . . . alive.

He parked the carryall next to the luxury automobile. Out of habit he noted the sun-yellow New Mexico license plate number on his clipboard. Then he jumped out to peer inside. "God almighty," he grunted.

With more haste than he usually exhibited, he transferred the unconscious boy from the front seat of the Lincoln to the carryall. He smoothed back the dark hair from the little forehead. The child's skin was red. And hot. Maybe 105 degrees, or more. No evident perspiration. Bad!

His mind was already working on fast-forward as he started up the car, setting the air conditioner at full blast. The nearest hogan, old Martha Two Goats's, was maybe ten miles to the west, close to the New Mexico border.

He steered toward the blue-gray mass of the Chuskas, following a seldom-used wagon track that wound through the summer growth of snakeweeds and gamma grass. Driving over fallen mesquite, rotted and half-buried in the sand, and plowing through the dunes, he urged the carryall up to thirty. Ahead vultures, perched on a dead goat, scattered. As they rode the air with their four-foot wingspread, their red eyes glared out of their black faces at him. Death was close on the heels of the carryall.

On a rise crowned by yellow paloverde trees stood an eight-sided hogan built of logs as the Navajo Way instructed, its single entrance facing east to the sunrise, and a smoke hole in the center of the roof. Behind it, he could see a mesquite-stake corral that contained huddled Churro sheep, whose wool was ideal for woven work, and in back of the corral stood a weathered plank shed. Empty. Old Martha and her granddaughters had probably taken the wagon into Window Rock. The shaggy collie she used to help her and her granddaughters herd the sheep came trotting out to the car, its tawny tail wagging happily.

Leaving the air conditioning running, he took the child from the carryall first. The boy was in greater danger of dying, but would also respond to first aid more quickly. He toted the shorts-clad child toward the well, which had been drilled by the federal government. A huge galvanized tank of water stood at the foot of an old wooden windmill. He plunged the boy into the lukewarm water. Reflexively, the child gasped. Droplets clung to his long, spiked lashes, and his lids snapped open momentarily to reveal his eyes. Blue. Pale blue. Dead eyes.

Instantly, he regretted the thought. It represented a slip back into the illogical hostility he had struggled against as a child himself.

He returned the wet boy to the front seat, then hefted the woman over his shoulder like a hundred pound burlap bag of Idaho pink beans, and lugged her to the tank. He submerged her in the water, and she came up sputtering.

While her arms thrashed at him ineffectually, his gaze strayed to her softly rounded body. Her wet linen skirt, the deep pink shade of the desert at dusk, clung suggestively to the curve of her hips.

Her eyes fired murderous salvos. A lethal snarl hissed from her cracked lips. A she-cat. Then she collapsed like a demolished building. He caught her under the arms before she sank beneath the three-foot-deep water, and hauled her back to the carry-all.

All his attention was riveted on her now, as he crouched beside her in the narrow space between the seats. As he disrobed her, her glinting wet hair skimmed the edge of his face, tickling his skin. Its fragrance was a siren's whisper. He found it difficult to work efficiently with the distraction of her.

First, the pantyhose, torn at the soles and a mass of runs. No panties. Then the skirt. Great legs. She had sturdy shoulders, but her ivory neck was fragile. He liked the human body: the texture of its skin over the firmness of bone. She had a woman's body, not the emaciated, bony look prevalent in the slick pages of fashion magazines. Her warm flesh felt soft, like an eiderdown quilt.

Still unconscious and entirely naked now, she shivered violently against the blast of refrigerated air. "Cold," she murmured. But her flesh was as hot as an electric blanket.

He carried her clothes back to the tank, resoaked them, so that they were dripping and heavy, then began wrapping them around her nude body. Goose bumps speckled her flesh. He draped the blouse over her breasts, his fingers brushing their full sides. He felt the scorching hunger invade his body, and self-disgust washed over him.

She moaned again. "Danny..."

The boy? "He's going to be all right," he said soothingly as he tucked the hem of her skirt under her hip. His fingers lingered briefly on the soft curve, then, as if burned, withdrew quickly to wrap the damp pantyhose about her throat. "Danny's going to be all right."

He made sure of that by disrobing the boy next and wrapping the child's wet clothing about his body.

Next he siphoned a small amount of gasoline from the carryall's tank to bathe the woman's lacerated hands. The wounds caused by the rusty wire were superficial, but he didn't believe in taking chances. It was always the insignificant things that tripped you up, that toppled kingdoms and laid waste to the best of plans.

As he patted a gasoline-dampened red flannel handkerchief over her palms, he noted her nails, short but well groomed. Capable hands. He liked that.

Her breath hissed in as the make-do antiseptic seared her wounds. "Sadist!" she breathed, and he had to grin.

"Who are you?" he asked her, wondering if she would respond to his question with an answer or an evasion.

Something furtive shadowed her eyes. "Lynn... Lynn Knight."

She was lying. He could tell. "You were crazy to get off I-40, lady."

She wouldn't meet his eyes. Her lids lowered. Beneath his fingers, the pulse in her wrist jumped. "...sightseeing."

"Well, you missed the Painted Desert by a good fifty miles."

She didn't answer, and he knew she had passed out again. He looked over the front seat. The fuel-gauge needle pointed to nearly empty. He would need the remaining gas to get to the BIA health clinic in the nearby Window Rock subagency. And if he ran out before he got there? He glanced back at her. No, the two of them would never make it.

His decision made, he once more picked her up, carrying her into the hogan this time. Against the wall were rolled up sheepskins for bedding. He unfurled one with a kick of his knee-high moccasin and laid her on the woolly length, re-tucking her wet clothing around her. Then he collected the boy and stretched him out on another sheepskin on the far side of the firepit. Hopefully Old Martha would return soon to take care of them.

For a long moment he stood, staring down at the woman. The sight of her made him recall all that he had left behind. Double-breasted blazers, razor-creased wool pants, tasseled loafers. The problem was that he had been one of a hundred thousand Identikit look-alikes.

And what had this woman been? A socialite? A mindless mannequin? She was on the run, he was sure of that. She was as jumpy as a virgin at a prison rodeo. What was she running from? Had she kidnapped the boy?

After he notified the Window Rock health clinic, he meant to drive on into Gallup. He would have the radio dispatcher at the BIA's Law and Order building run a check on the Lincoln's license plate.

He pushed back his baseball cap. He had a suspicion that the Arizona Highway Patrol, the Apache County State Sheriff, the FBI, the Navajo police and the BIA were all going to descend like a swarm of buzzards on a place that was legally under only tribal-federal jurisdiction.

It was going to be one hell of a party.

Chapter Two

The first thing Jaclyn Richardson saw when she opened her eyes was an old woman whose face looked like a relief map of New Mexico. Lumps of turquoise were suspended from heavy earlobes by leather strings, and blue-black hair heavily streaked with gray was bound at either side of her head in squash-blossom fashion by red wool yarn. The woman's emerald-green velveteen blouse provided the only other color in the darkness of the room. Solemnly she stared down at Jaclyn with rock-brown eyes hooded by sloping lids; then she clicked her tongue against a silver front tooth, as if satisfied, and waddled away.

Where am I?

Frantically, Jaclyn glanced around the room. She had entered a time warp. Dirt floors, no running water, no signs of electricity. Round walls. She was in a hogan. A hole in the center of the roof allowed the only light, a thin shaft of dust-hazed sunlight, to enter. It spotlighted the old Indian woman, who had gone to kneel on the other side of the firepit. Danny was lying there, propped up on one elbow, staring around, looking as dazed as Jaclyn felt.

The old woman laid her hand on his forehead, then nodded broadly. "Very good!"

"Mama!" Danny cried. The sparkle was back in his sweet blue eyes, but she noted worriedly that the freckles on his abnormally pale face had been washed away, like the stones and brush in Kaibeto Wash after a desert flood.

Wrapping the sheepskin blanket around him, he scrambled over to her and buried himself within her outstretched arms. She gathered him next to her and rained kisses on his forehead. It was blessedly cool. "I love you...love you so much," she whispered. She had been so close to losing him, to never seeing him again.

In a flood of memory, it all came back to her. She had been running away. The Navajo Indian Reservation, where the state had no jurisdiction, had seemed the safest place. That was foolish, of course, because she couldn't hide out here forever. But she had been frenzied with fear that Todd would find her and take Danny from her. Her ex-husband's parting words had been, "If the cops don't get you, I will."

Todd Richardson held several prominent New Mexico officials in the palm of his well-greased hand, and his credo was, "There is no right or wrong. There is only what is possible." Too late, she had learned that the handsome playboy she had married was a spoiled mama's boy. He had always been just a bit too handsome. His laugh was probably the best thing about him: wicked and uninhibited and charming—and totally false. She realized sadly that she had become cynical since marrying Todd.

Another image superimposed itself over that of her husband's. A man's face, but not nearly as plastic-handsome. It was a strong, wind-burned face, filled with unmistakable kindness. A broken nose... generous lips that twitched with self mockery... and eyes that were bright with humor. Pure gray, slate gray. "Hunter's eyes," her grandfather had called them, "the color of a true marksman."

More than the man's features, she remembered the gentle hands that had cared for her and Danny, if being dunked under water could be called gentle. But then she vaguely recalled the way he had draped her refreshingly wet clothing over her feverish body. She realized that he had seen her naked, and she felt the heat of a blush scald her cheeks.

A breech clout and a baseball cap?

Could he—and all that she thought he had done—have been a mirage, like the water on the road? Feeling very foolish, she asked the old woman, "A man...wearing a breech clout and a blue baseball cap...did he bring Danny and me here?"

"Joe Watchman." The Indian woman gave Danny a plastic glass that was chipped and clouded by time and use. "Joe Watchman, he brought you here, I betcha."

"Joe Watchman?" The name told Jaclyn nothing. "Who is Joe Watchman?"

"Joe Watchman," said a girlish voice from somewhere else in the hogan, "is just probably the toughest *hombre* between here and Albuquerque."

Jaclyn turned, looking for the child who owned the voice. She found her farther back in the hogan, near a loom used to weave wool. She was a thin girl, maybe ten years old, with enormous coal-black eyes. Her mouth was a perfect cupid's bow that looked accustomed to merriment. Hiding behind the loom was another girl, younger, maybe five or six, a replica of the older one. She put her tiny hand over her mouth and giggled.

Could these two girls possibly be the daughters of the old Indian woman? Women out here aged more quickly because of their exposure to the fierce elements: the dry summer heat that turned skin into leather; the icy winter cold that compounded the wrinkles. But even taking that into consideration, this woman appeared to be far past childbearing age.

"Lieutenant Joe Watchman," continued the older girl, placing emphasis on the man's rank, "captured a rabid sheep dog barehanded."

"Wow!" Danny said.

The Indian woman took the glass he had drained from him, refilled it with water from a clay *olla* and passed it to Jaclyn. The water was marvelously cool.

"And he punched a bad guy in the nose," the younger girl chimed in, galvanized by Danny's sudden interest. "Punched him out cold. I saw it happen."

"The man was an escaped convict, Tessa," the older sister reproved. "And it was his mouth. Knocked out three of his front teeth."

"You don't know everything, Gracie Tsinnijinnie," Tessa shot back, but the ends of her rosy lips were tilted gaily upward, as if her genes had formed them that way permanently and unalterably.

Like Danny, Jaclyn was captivated by the two sisters and their yarns about this Joe Watchman. He was obviously their hero. "Well, will Joe Watchman be coming back soon? I'd like to thank him for rescuing us."

And get back to my car. If this elusive Joe Watchman could have chanced upon her so easily, then Todd could very well have, too.

"Oh, yes," Gracie said in a very adult manner. "Joe Watchman will come back. A BIA detective never forgets anyone or anything."

"A BIA detective?" Jaclyn felt as if a beehive had been emptied into her stomach. She jerked back the sheepskin blanket, then remembered that she was absolutely naked. She looked at the old woman. "Mrs...."

"Old Martha," the Navajo woman supplied, grinning.

"Old Martha. Please, can I have my clothes?"

"They're still drying," Gracie said, pointing to a willow rack just behind the loom.

"That doesn't matter." Holding the blanket around herself, Jaclyn got to her feet. Her knees were wobbly, but adrenaline was charging through her bloodstream. Between this Joe Watchman's Indian instincts and his law enforcement background, he represented an immediate danger to Danny and her.

"Please," she said, turning with a pleading look to the old woman. "I have to leave here. Now. I...I have an appointment I have to keep in...in Flagstaff." Only at that moment did she make up her mind where she was going, and it wasn't Flagstaff.

At first she had simply been running, but perhaps not as blindly as she had thought. Back to Kaibeto. That was where she would go. Her grandfather was long dead, but... She didn't finish the thought, because she really wasn't ready to make a decision yet. Just keeping one step ahead of her wily ex-husband required all her mental faculties. And she was tired, so tired, and weak and frightened and helpless.

The old woman watched her with a stolid expression, then, ignoring her plea, waddled over to the fire to stir the contents of a kettle. The savory smell, lamb stew, floating in fat and boiled corn, reached Jaclyn, conjuring up images that had long been forgotten, images of times she had once been anxious to put behind her. With those images came the suspicion that the old woman probably hadn't understood everything she had said.

Urgently, Jaclyn tried to recall whatever Navajo words she had learned, but only the standard greeting of "Ya-ta-hey" and a few other simple phrases came to her. The Navajo language was a series of nasal intonations, with the pitch having as much, or more, to do with what was being said as the actual words. Her grandfather, his voice rustling like the pages of a well-loved old book, had once told her that because Navajo was an extremely difficult language to master, Navajo "Code Talkers" had been used in World War II to prevent the Japanese from interpreting U.S. secret military messages.

She turned to the two sisters, who had obviously learned English at an Indian boarding school. Sitting on the back of her heels, so that she was at their eye level, she asked, "Will you ask your mother if there's any way I can get back to my car?"

Gracie shook her head, and her pigtails flopped against her shoulders. "We don't know where your car is. You were already here when we returned from Window Rock."

Great. "How far are we from Window Rock?"

Gracie pursed her lips, Navajo fashion. "Five miles, maybe."

To the Navajo, a mile could be a block, or it could be ten miles. It all depended on how far the lips jutted out, and Jaclyn had never learned to judge that. Few Anglos ever did. Jaclyn calculated that she was probably within fifteen miles of Window Rock. But which way?

Worse, the awful realization occurred to her that she couldn't reclaim her car even if she had been able to get to it. By now the intrepid Joe Watchman would have the police going over it with microscopic precision. They would track her down. At that moment she didn't know whether to bless the mysterious Joe Watchman or curse him. True, he had saved her life—and Danny's. But Joe Watchman could very well be the instrument that would take Danny out of her life.

For her, losing Danny would be the same as signing her death warrant.

"Why are we going to Flagstaff, Mom?" asked Danny. He was still wrapped in his sheepskin, his chin propped on his palm. He was totally fascinated by the unusual place and people. She had never told him much about her earlier life. That had been a mistake, she realized now.

"To sightsee. You know—Grand Canyon, the big meteor crater, things like that. It will be a sort of a mini-vacation." She tried to keep her tone casual, pleasant, but, in truth, she was panicky. "Does a bus run near here?" she asked Gracie.

"Uh-huh. Over on the Interstate, but that's forty, fifty miles or so. A long, long way."

Gracie's lips were screwed up as if she had just tasted a persimmon. I-40 had to be quite some distance away then. Jaclyn felt defeat lapping at her, but she wasn't about to give up docilely. "Do you have a car—or a pickup—that I could rent? I'll pay—"

Suddenly she realized that she didn't have her purse with her. She had left it somewhere in the desert, along with her shoes.

Now what was she going to do? She had no money, no credit cards, and she was marooned in a log hogan, with precious time running out. As if reading her thoughts, the Indian woman squatted next to a small cedar chest and pulled out an object. "Yours? I find it beside you."

"My purse! Oh, yes, thank you." She took the alligator bag and fished inside for her wallet. No doubt Joe Watchman had gone through it and checked her identification.

The older sister came to stand before her. Draped over her arms were Jaclyn's skirt and blouse. The child's black eyes, on a level with Jaclyn's own, were wise, despite her youthful face. "My grandmother says it is dangerous for you to leave today without resting some more."

It's more dangerous if I don't leave. "Danny and I really feel much better."

She went behind the loom and speedily began to dress. The damp blouse and skirt chilled her skin.

"My grandmother says you should wait to travel until after sundown. The heat . . ."

Oh, yes, the heat. She could already feel the heat of Joe Watchman hot on her heels.

"I really must go. This appointment is very important."

She took Danny's plaid shorts and lemon-yellow T-shirt from the rack. "Get dressed, Danny. Quickly."

Looking like a child king in his coronation robe, her son pulled the heavy sheepskin along with him, scurrying for the concealment of the loom.

She turned back to Gracie. "Does your grandmother have a car or a pickup I could borrow? Anything? It doesn't matter how old. I'd only need it for a day or so, until I could rent a car. Then I'd see that it was returned."

Gracie said something to Old Martha in those intonations that baffled Jaclyn. The woman's wizened face turned toward Jaclyn. For a long moment the old Indian woman scrutinized her, and Jaclyn knew that there was nothing she could do to convince the woman to trust her. Old Martha would make up her own mind.

At last she nodded solemnly; then a silver tooth gleamed in her mouth. "Yabetcha."

Relief numbed Jaclyn's raw nerve endings, until Tessa said, "A buckboard. We have a buckboard."

"A buckboard?" Jaclyn repeated in a dazed voice.

"Yes," Gracie said, explaining. "We hitch Mona and Lisa to the buckboard whenever we need to go anywhere."

Well, she needed to go somewhere. Anywhere to get away from the hogan and Joe Watchman. "Danny, let's go."

Totally engrossed, he was watching as Tessa peered at him from one side of the loom, then the other. His

freckles were beginning to surface again, signifying
the return of his health. She remembered when he
had contracted meningitis last year, how frightened
she had been and how washed-out his freckles had
become. She was still frightened. "Danny," she repeated, more insistent this time. "We have to go!"

The gap-toothed grin appealed to her maternal
instincts. "Mom, I'm hungry. Can we eat first?"

They *did* need to eat. Their bodies' systems had
been depleted, and she felt so weak that simple decision making seemed an arduous task. But they
didn't have time.

"Frybread," the old woman said, pointing to the
skillet at one side of the firepit. "Take it with you."

So, the Indian woman understood more than she
let on. Grateful, Jaclyn said, "Yes, please. That's
very kind of you. We would like that."

Despite the hospitality of the woman and her
granddaughters, Jaclyn couldn't leave the hogan
quickly enough. Warm frybread in hand, she and
Danny trailed the old woman out to a shed behind a
corral full of bleating sheep. Gracie ran ahead to let
down the wooden gate where two ragged-looking
burros stood placidly. Then she led them out of the
shed and began hitching them to a buckboard that
had seen better days.

With rapt attention, Danny watched the older girl
work with the harness and reins. Once again Jaclyn

realized that there was so much that Danny had
missed out on in the overly protected and con-
stricted environment in which she and Todd had
raised him. He knew which silverware to use at a
formal dinner, but he didn't know the rudiments of
self-sufficiency. He would never know how to survive on his own if the occasion called for it.

Survive. She glanced up at the sky. The blinding
sun was nearing the four o'clock point in the white-
hot sky. How long since Joe Watchman had left her
and Danny at the hogan? How long until he returned for them?

After Gracie finished harnessing the burros to the
wagon, the Indian woman rattled off something in
that unfathomable language. Gracie replied, then
turned to Jaclyn. "My grandmother wants to know
if you know how to handle burros and a buckboard?"

"Enough to get me where I'm going." Actually,
she had been at the reins of a buckboard only once,
and her grandfather had been a reassuring presence
beside her, ready to take the reins if she decided to
abdicate her position as driver. She did know that
burros could be recalcitrant creatures when the whim
took them. "I'll see that the buckboard is returned
to your grandmother by tomorrow."

What she planned to do was head for Window
Rock, the headquarters of the Navajo Nation, in ef-

fect, the Indian Washington, D.C. There she could hire someone to return the wagon to Old Martha and her granddaughters. Perhaps she could hide out in Window Rock, at least until she got her head on straight and decided what would be best for Danny and her. She realized now that, however tempting the idea was, she couldn't go to Kaibeto, where she had been heading instinctively. Todd might think to look for her there.

She hadn't talked to him much about those years. At the time when they had met, she had wanted only to escape reservation life, and she certainly hadn't wanted any reminders of those years. Later on she didn't bother to bring up her past very often, mainly because she didn't think Todd, or his kind of people, would understand.

"You don't have to worry about getting the buckboard back to us," Gracie said. "Just slap Mona and Lisa on their rumps when you're finished. They'll find their way back to our hogan."

When Jaclyn tried to give Old Martha some money—three dollars, all she had, besides some loose change—the Navajo woman wouldn't take it. Yes, this was the way Jaclyn remembered the people of the Navajo Reservation. They had a generosity of the soul that was boundless. But too often they were also full of suspicion and stupidity and self-pity.

She set off in the direction where Gracie told her she would find Highway 264 and Window Rock, though she certainly didn't plan to use the highway. If she did, there was too much chance she might encounter the Indian detective. Window Rock couldn't be far. She would travel during the rest of the evening, while it was cool, if the burros kept behaving as well as they were at the moment.

"Hey, Mom, this is great!" Danny said at her side, his mouth full of the last of his frybread.

She grinned down at him. "I used to pig out on that stuff."

"When you lived with your grandfather?"

"Yes." She forestalled any more questions, questions she wasn't ready to answer yet, by saying, "Give me my half of that frybread, young man. I'm hungry, too, you know."

"Could I drive the wagon, Mom?"

"Sure, cricket. Hold the lines firmly in your palms. Like this," she said as she showed him.

Overhead the sky was as blue as water, as deep as turquoise set in a silver conch hat band. She would almost have enjoyed the ride—like an afternoon outing—if she hadn't been so worried about Joe Watchman. An Indian could track a spider across the sand.

She wished the burros would go faster, but both she and Danny were unaccustomed to handling them, so maybe slower was better. What if they bolted, dragging the buckboard with them over the deceptively flat land? Why couldn't she just learn to enjoy the present moment, the beauty of it, the way the Navajos did? Instead, during the past few years she had joined Todd in the white man's habit of racing against time for achievement, for progress, for recognition.

After she finished her share of the frybread, she took over at the reins. A little sigh of relief escaped her when she picked up the indelible traces of a wagon road. In the brutal sunlight the windblown patterns of red sand contrasted with the jagged lava rocks and the dark stone strewn across the area by violent volcanic activity a thousand years ago.

A hot wind rose, playing with her hair, whipping it across her face. Impatiently she tucked the strands behind one ear. Hot wind, hot sun, hot sand. She had forgotten those things, also.

The terrain seemed as flat as a drumhead, but she knew how illusory the land was. Ahead, she watched the sky narrow into a blue wedge between canyon walls. Good, it would be cooler there, she thought.

It wasn't. There was shadow, but no shade. The canyon walls radiated an enervating heat that seared the windpipe and lungs.

She couldn't let herself get lost, get trapped in some canyon where she couldn't see the track of the stars across the heavens later in the evening, couldn't watch the star the Navajos called Hotomkam travel westward.

She tried not to worry about the consequences of getting lost. The first time, yesterday, she had been fleeing in a mind-numbing panic. Now she was trying to think ahead, to prepare. If she kept heading due west... just ten miles or so, maybe... if she grew thirsty, she had only to look for a tamarisk tree... wherever a tamarisk stood there was bound to be water. Cactus pulp would have moisture, too. Those cactus flowers, white and fleshy and almost fluorescent, that gave off a sweet, musky odor... She really didn't have to worry... Her hands were beginning to ache from gripping the reins, and her back was hurting from the jouncing of the wagon.

"Mom, I'm tired."

"Climb in the back and lie down, cricket. We'll sleep in a real bed tonight." *I hope.*

A faint purple was coloring the canyon walls. The shadows of leafless bushes played tricks with her eyesight. The monotonous clip-clop of the burros' hooves dulled her senses. Several times she glanced over her shoulder, half expecting to see a spiral of dust to indicate that she was being followed. Her fear made her feel irrational, as if she could feel the warm breath of Joe Watchman fanning the back of her neck.

Immediately ahead of the burros glided the shadow of a swooping hawk, trying to catch the rise of a hot air current. She found herself wanting to do that, too, to swoop and soar on the thermals and fly away where Todd and Joe Watchman couldn't come. I'm tired, too, she thought. Bone weary. All the months and years of fighting Todd and his willful determination to do whatever he wanted, regardless of whether she and Danny might need him, had left her spirit drained. At the moment she wanted nothing more than to curl up in the back of the wagon alongside Danny.

The shadow that fell across the narrow range of her vision didn't seep into her consciousness at first. But as the shadow moved steadily with the buckboard's shadow, her perception that she and Danny were not alone grew. The shadow was accompanied by a low humming sound. The bees that had seemed to swarm in her stomach were back, swarming in her ears, this time.

With an effort she turned her gaze to the left, in the direction of the humming, but the blinding sun hid the face of the phantom who drove at her side. Still, she knew who he was. She had been expecting him all this time. It was as if she had waited for him forever.

She had known he would find her.

Chapter Three

Lady, you sure are into masochism.''

She was headed for another heat stroke if she stayed out in the sun another hour. Obviously she wasn't interested in that possibility.

He watched her stare dully down at him. Behind him, his carryall blocked the buckboard's way. Slowly she lifted a hand, as if the effort were costing her her last ounce of strength, and brushed back the dark hair the searing wind had tumbled across her blistered lips. Her sunburnt face was drawn, her hair matted. Her expensive linen skirt and silk blouse were wrinkled like a washboard.

Still, she had class. The sunset was gold on her skin, red gold in her hair, and bathed the warm tones of her eyes and lips.

If the FBI rap sheet he had picked up in his office In basket was anything to go by, her ex-husband's family had long since diversified beyond New Mexico oil. Now the money was woven everywhere in the fabric of America: in cattle, long-term treasury bills, in Manhattan office blocks. The Richardson share of one computer company alone could wipe out the deficit of a small banana republic.

She said nothing, and he knew she was on the edge of hysteria. She was a woman who had been pushed to her limit. He held up his hand. "It's all right. Come on down from the buckboard. No one's going to harm you or your kid. Danny," he added. Hit the personal side, the Organization always stressed. The Organization, as the FBI preferred to call itself, could take a flying leap, he thought now.

When she made no motion to place her hand in his, he wrapped his hands around her waist. An hourglass waist. Something about her seemed old-fashioned, despite her sophisticated trappings. Gently, as if dealing with a nervous mare, he lifted her down from the buckboard seat. And then all hell broke loose.

Her teeth were bared, her hands balled into fists. "I won't go back!" she exploded.

He caught the hand that lashed out at him awkwardly, then the other. With her wrists locked in one of his hands, he could feel her pulse pounding pitifully against her delicate blue-veined skin. He assured her quietly, "You don't have to go back. I promise."

She didn't hear him. "I won't give Danny up. Ever. You'll have to kill me first!"

She tried to twist away. But it was a futile motion. She was too small, her strength no match for his. But all his sympathy for her vanished when she jammed a knee up toward his most vulnerable area. She was so short—five foot three, according to her driver's license—that she missed him by a long shot. But her next kick was much better aimed and caught him in the shin.

That did it. He wrapped his arms around her body in a bear hug, then jerked her up against his chest while she vented her rage. Crying. Screaming. Her legs thrashed wildly, inches above the ground. She was a mother lioness protecting her cub, her eyes and mouth narrowed in fury and fear—powerful emotions that intensified her strength a hundredfold.

He subdued her the best way he knew how. The way he had wanted to from the very beginning. His mouth closed over hers. Her hissing scream was blocked in her throat, and surprise took the place of her anger. He was surprised, too, the strength of his own reaction catching him unprepared.

Her fury-rigid body went slack, and he took unfair advantage of her momentary surrender to prolong the kiss. His mouth moved over her lips, back and forth, with a delicately questing pressure. Her lips had the taste of sunheated silk under his—and panic. He could feel her racing heartbeat.

Some remnant of sensitivity reached through to him. Still holding her above the ground, he ended the kiss reluctantly. He smoothed the tangled hair, damp with tears, from her face. Her flush—from either pleasure or alarm—hit him with a powerful and disturbing force.

"It's all right," he said quietly, not knowing what other words to use. She was so skittish. "You're safe. You and your son."

"How can I trust you?" Her voice was a whisper of raw agony.

He set her feet on the ground and stepped back. The wind caught her skirt, moving it across his legs in a caress. "Do you have any choice?"

He watched her start to fall apart again, then pull herself back together. Her flush faded, leaving her dead white as she demanded, "What do you want from me?"

"I want to help you."

That surprised him, too. Officially, he had no responsibility for this woman—or for the boy with the pale blue eyes. The day was turning out to be full of surprises. He had almost driven over a half-naked woman at mid-morning, then ended up obligating himself to a wild Valkyrie at sunset. Maybe the BIA field supervisor was right. Maybe he should go back to the Organization.

"You know I lied to you about my name, don't you?" she asked softly.

She had such wonderful eyes. Her emotions found eloquent expression in them. Unknowingly, they pleaded. Unknowingly, they touched him. "You're Jaclyn Richardson. Anything else you want to tell me?"

"How do I know you won't take Danny away from me and turn him over to my husband?"

He squinted up at the copper sun. Still an hour to sunset, and as hot as a Navajo sweat lodge. South Dakota and all that snow and ice didn't seem so bad right now. "Because," he said with infinite patience, "there is no reason for me to take your son from you. After you stole your son from your ex-husband—"

"Stole?"

Good, she was responding. He noticed that her hands were clenched at her sides again. The tracks of her tears had dried, leaving clean paths down her dusty face. Still, she looked as if she was going to be all right. He crossed his arms and waited for her anger to take its natural course.

"I had custody of Danny! My ex-husband kidnapped him from me! I merely hired a private detective to find Todd and Danny, then went to Houston to reclaim what was mine."

"Right, ma'am. After you reclaimed him, your ex-husband tried to persuade the Houston police to pursue you. But what you don't know is that when the police learned you had custody, they abandoned the chase. You can return to Albuquerque now."

"That just shows how little you know, Lieutenant Joe Watchman!"

So, she knew who he was.

She spun on those silly spiked alligator heels and stalked back to the wagon. He was getting tired of going after her, he thought. Phil Tames-the-Horse had reported a stolen pickup, and he needed to get over there to investigate the incident.

In one easy stride he caught up with her. His hand lapped around her upper arm. Rounded, firm flesh. Soft as velvet. The wind flicked her hair across his chin and mouth, and he caught her fragrance, a siren's whisper. The blood rushed through his body, leaving him tingling all over.

"Look, lady, there's not going to be any child left for your ex-husband to kidnap if you go off half-

cocked on your own again." His words had come out
snappish and irritable. He was impatient with her
willfulness, and annoyed with himself for being fascinated by her.

However, his statement seemed to get through to
her. She looked down at the fingers that gripped her
arm, then back up at his face. For a long time she
studied it. As an Indian would. Looking for the soul.
He said nothing, but met her eyes with his, yielding
to her this once, letting her search as deeply as she
dared, until her head lowered in submission.

"All right," she whispered.

"Fine. Get in the carryall." He didn't trust himself to touch her again. "I'll get the boy."

The child was, amazingly, asleep, but his skin was
hot. Joe plowed his fingers through Danny's rumpled hair. He felt perspiration on the scalp. Good, he
wasn't dehydrating—yet.

After he stretched the boy out on the carryall's
back seat, he led the burros around full circle, until
they were facing west, toward the hogan. Then he
whacked them on their sweaty rumps. "Git!" They
took off at a trot, dust from their hooves powdering
the air.

When he joined the woman in the front, she sat as
far away from him as she could. He started up the
engine. "Are you thirsty? I picked up a couple of

bottles of beer on my way out of Window Rock. And some soda for your boy.''

He had also picked up a box of salt tablets at the BIA health clinic, since Pamela had been out on an emergency call. He had figured that Jaclyn Richardson might decide to hightail it across the desert again, and he had been right.

She didn't answer him. She seemed to be staring out the window at nothing in particular, though even after four years in New Mexico, he still found his gaze drawn to the banded pink-and-buff pinnacles and mesas.

He said nothing else, but simply waited. Ahead of the carryall a jackrabbit dashed across the wagon tracks at the last possible second. He could tell that she saw it, but she said nothing. Joe always found it interesting to watch a white try to be silent. Silence could be informative. She caught her bottom lip between her teeth. Three minutes later, she unconsciously wrung her hands together. Nervously, she shoved her hair back behind one delicately fluted ear. A diamond stud glinted there.

At last the silence got to her. "Where are we going?" she demanded.

He grinned. "First to the Public Health Clinic at Window Rock. I want Pamela—the Health Service nurse there—to take a look at you two. Then, after we stop by my office in Gallup and notify the State

Police to take you and Danny off their missing persons list, we'll pick up your car. I left it at the impound—''

She turned on him. A curtain of dark hair, lit by subtle glints the red of an autumn oak leaf, swung angrily against her shoulders. Yet there was something beseeching in the gray-green depths of her eyes. ''Listen,'' she pleaded, ''you don't know Todd...my ex-husband...like I do. He won't give up that easily.''

''Then tell me about him.''

She shot him an assessing look, as if she were seeing him—really seeing him—for the first time. ''Don't you ever take that baseball cap off?''

He laughed. ''You don't appreciate my sartorial originality?''

''I don't imagine,'' she said dryly, ''that anyone has the courage to ask someone as big as you are to remove his hat. Especially a Navajo on his own home turf.''

''I'm a Cheyenne.''

''That explains your height,'' she murmured, almost to herself. ''But what are you doing in—''

''You were going to tell me about your husband?''

Her gaze slid away from him. ''Todd. Yes. If you meet him, you come away impressed. He's the Mr. Congeniality of the country club set. And he's shrewd. But at thirty-two he's just a spoiled boy. He thinks that because of his family's money and influence, he's above the law. *And he is*, Lieutenant Watchman!"

"To begin with, I'd suggest placing a restraint order against him."

"You don't understand! He owns people. Brownley, the judge. Richter, the—"

"The state attorney general?"

"Yes. And several state congressmen, in addition to a federal supreme court judge. The law means nothing to him. It was written for the masses, the plebeians! Todd will find me, and whatever it takes, whatever he has to do, he'll take Danny away from me again."

"If he loves your son that much, doesn't he want what's best for him?"

A tight smile pulled at her lips. "He wants me back. Danny is his hostage."

This was getting more interesting by the moment. "You want to explain that?"

Exasperatedly, she blew at a strand of wayward hair that had fallen across her sunburnt nose. "He doesn't love Danny. Danny is competition for Todd, don't you see?" She flicked him an impatient glance. "There can be only one boy in the Richardson family. Todd is the perennial boy—with his boyish smile! Dear God, I was so blind!"

She glanced out her window, but not before he saw the mist of agony in her eyes. "My leaving him proves to the world that he's less than perfect. If he can make me come back, if he can force me to re-marry him, he'll have won. He'll have shown the world how perfect and irresistible he is." The caustic tone of her voice faded at the end of her statement.

"Could be he loves you." He would love someone like her, with that spirit, that indomitability.

"Please..." She put her hand over her eyes, her fingers massaging her brow. After a moment she said, "He keeps a string of mistresses. At various times I've begged him to give them up or... give me up. But our divorce hurts the family's image."

"And this doesn't?"

With a burst of nearly hysterical laughter, she looked up at him. "Of course not. Because this will never be allowed to make the papers, or the T.V. and radio networks. It'll all be hush-hushed once my husband's family learns about it. They couldn't tolerate having the family name tarnished by such a common thing as a domestic squabble. Please believe me, Lieutenant Watchman. Danny and I have to keep out of his way until..."

"Until what?"

Abruptly, she buried her face in her hands and wept softly. "I don't know," she mumbled. "I don't know. And I'm so tired."

Her crying made him uncomfortable. He shifted on the seat, watching a tumbleweed bounce across the wagon tracks up ahead. She meant trouble for him. Without being able to define why, he knew it was true.

Regretting it all the way, he said, "Look, after you get a clean bill of health, you and the kid can put up at a fishing cabin I have up in the Chuskas. Up at Whiskey Lake. Until you get your head on straight. Until you make up your mind what you want to do. No one is going to find you up there."

Window Rock, Jaclyn thought, looked a lot like Tuba City, the headquarters of the Western Navajo Agency, just somewhat bigger. The dying sun cast a kind light on the Navajo capital. The squat little town was backed into the blue shadows of an orange-red escarpment humped on the horizon—an immense monolith of red sandstone through which time, wind and water had worn a large hole, the window that gave the town its name.

A few elm trees shaded the native stone houses, tarpaper shacks and dilapidated stores. An outsider would find little of beauty in a place like this, but her grandfather had taught her to love the warm colors of the earth, the people, the wide-open skies—as blue as the baseball cap Lieutenant Joe Watchman wore.

From beneath her lashes she studied the big Indian surreptitiously while he drove through town. In the sideways angle of the setting sun his face was as harsh as sandstone. How old was he? She tried to guess, but it was difficult, with the baseball cap hiding his hair and shadowing his features. Maybe thirty? Thirty-five, she finally decided.

His hand on the steering wheel was broad, with strong blunt fingers, two of them crooked. Even sitting down, he looked tall. His baseball cap just barely cleared the truck's ceiling. Probably six-foot-five or so, with a good 225 pounds on his solid frame. His shoulders went on forever. A steely sheet of muscle sheathed his bare chest and stomach. Her glance halted at the leather band of the breech clout and skidded away to study the original tribal buildings of red sandstone that slid by outside her window.

Nevertheless, the memory of him stayed with her. She recalled how gracefully—and silently—he had moved. Yet his grace could in no way be associated with femininity. He was pure masculinity. Raw sexuality.

She felt a flush searing her face at the direction her thoughts were taking. The sharp spots of heat in her cheeks turned to ice as she remembered her marriage. Joe Watchman was a man, and after Todd, she felt as if she might never trust a man again. She supposed it was Joe Watchman's gentleness that was getting to her. It had been so long, so very long, since anyone had shown her any tenderness, any affection. She had known eleven years of marriage, eleven years of hurried lovemaking in which the precious communication between two souls had been sacrificed for those fleeting seconds of finality.

"This is it," Joe Watchman said, parking in front of a small, brown basalt building. "The BIA clinic."

A frightening thought struck her, and she reached out to touch his arm, then immediately withdrew her fingers from the sun-heated, bronzed flesh. Her gesture had seemed so intimate. He was a perfect stranger, and yet . . .

He glanced down at her hands, which were now locked together in her lap. His lips flexed but didn't quite lift into a smile. "Yes?"

"This health service nurse—Pamela—she'll have to make a report on treating Danny and me. If that report gets out, Todd will—"

"It won't. Pamela owes me one."

Jaclyn shuddered with the force of her relief.

Pamela was a young woman of twenty-five or so, with angular features and an angular body. She had faded blond hair and wore faded blue jeans. The desert sun did that, Jaclyn thought. It bleached everything. Bleached people, bleached emotions, bleached hope. Now she remembered one of the reasons why she had fled the reservation and its unforgiving desert.

The nurse's eyes, though, were dark—a dark brown—and they studied Jaclyn carefully, weighing her up as another female. They casually dismissed her and returned to settle on the BIA agent's face. The fact that he wore only a breech clout didn't seem to faze the woman in the least. "Well, what have you brought me, Joe? More lost souls?"

Jaclyn didn't like the way she said those last words. Almost unconsciously, she drew closer to Danny—and Joe Watchman.

"Heatstroke victims." He glanced down at Danny, who stirred sleepily in his arms. "The kid looks like he's going to be all right, but I'd like you to give him and his mother a health check anyway."

The nurse nodded briskly. Her hair, gathered at the nape of her neck by a tortoiseshell clasp, swayed against her back. "Bring them into the examination room."

Aftershock might have left Jaclyn fatigued, but she figured she could understand directions without having to be led like an animal. Pamela's attitude irritated her, but she realized that her irritation was a normal part of the emotional pattern following shock.

With an effort she repressed her irrational annoyance and followed the nurse and the BIA detective past an empty admitting room and around a corner into a small, sterile-green cubicle. Shiny stainless steel instruments glinted under the bright fluorescent lights. An antiseptic smell permeated the air.

Joe Watchman laid Danny on the paper-covered examination table, and she leaned over her son. "Danny," she said, ruffling his hair affectionately. "Wake up, cricket."

He rubbed at his sleepy eyes, and his slowly awakening yawn displayed three missing teeth that had impoverished the tooth fairy. He looked around the room, taking in the strange man and woman; then his blue eyes, wide with uncertainty, sought her out. "Is this where we're staying tonight, Mom?"

She tried a reassuring smile. This had to be bewildering to him. First Todd had kidnapped him for three weeks and hauled him to Houston. She had been so frantic, not knowing whether Danny was all right. Then, after an aging private detective had located him for her, she had taken Danny back and carted him all over creation. It didn't seem fair to her son, this push-and-pull tug-of-war. But, dear God, she didn't know what else to do. She just wanted Danny to be loved as Todd never could love him, had never loved him. He deserved that much. She only hoped that children were as resilient as the child psychologists claimed.

"We're not there yet. This is a nurse, and she just wants to make sure we're all right."

Danny looked at the young woman warily, and Joe Watchman said, "She's like the nurse at your school, Danny."

"Who are you?" Danny asked with a cautious glance up at the big man.

Jaclyn stiffened, dreading his reply. *A detective...policeman...special agent...hunting you and your mother down.*

"A fisherman. How about you?"

Before Danny could answer, Pamela stepped in front of him. "Open your mouth, Danny. I need to take your temperature." Efficiently, but with less warmth than a freezer attendant, she inserted the thermometer beneath his tongue and glanced at her utilitarian watch. Next she took his pulse and blood pressure, noted them on a chart, then did the same to Jaclyn.

When she finished, she asked how long Jaclyn and Danny had been exposed to the direct desert heat. Jaclyn noticed that Pamela addressed her question toward Joe Watchman, not herself, and in a very deferential manner.

The woman was in love with him!

Jaclyn eyed the Indian. Arms folded laconically, he was watching the nurse, but saying nothing himself. Jaclyn remembered her first summer at Kaibeto, how difficult she had found it to talk to the boarding school Indians who spoke English. The white man's custom of expecting a listener to do more than listen was contrary to the courteous Navajo custom. It had taken two or three misunderstandings before she had finally understood that the Navajo required no reassurance that you were listening while they talked.

"You seem to have pulled them through the ordeal just fine, Joe. The woman has some burns and needs a medicated ointment applied to her skin. Otherwise, I only need to keep them here overnight for observation. Just as a precautionary measure."

Jaclyn realized she had never thanked the Indian detective for saving herself and Danny, but she couldn't worry about that lapse of courtesy now. She picked up her purse from the examination table. Only fear-fueled adrenaline supported her legs; otherwise she would have collapsed from sheer physical and mental exhaustion.

"Sorry," she said with a wintery smile to the other two, "but Danny and I are leaving. We're here for a vacation, not hospital confinement."

Joe Watchman stepped between her and Danny. She looked up into his ruggedly handsome face. "We can't stay here," she said, her words distinct and spaced for emphasis. Her expression said, Don't try to stop us.

His eyes hoarded light like newly-minted coins. He nodded, ever so slightly, then looked past her to the nurse. "They're staying with me, Pamela. I'll keep an eye on them."

"Oh? Do you think that's wise?" She fidgeted with the file folder she had set up on Danny and Jaclyn, then said testily, "Well, you'll have to sign out, saying you're taking them into your care. Are you sure you want that much responsibility on your hands?"

He reached around Jaclyn and took the folder from Pamela. He ripped it into halves, fourths, eighths, and finally into shreds. Jaclyn saw the sharpness in his smile, but his tone was good-natured. "You never treated these two, Pamela. All right?"

Chapter Four

As they ascended the Zuni foothills, the temperature began to drop. Joe turned the heater on low. A rising moon illuminated copses of junipers. Jaclyn stared at them, then absently stroked Danny's hair. His head on her lap, he was stretched out between her and Lieutenant Watchman, asleep. She was so tired, but her lids wouldn't close. If she went to sleep... if she didn't keep a painful vigil... if she relaxed her guard—Todd would find her and Danny.

Worse, had she jumped from the frying pan into the fire by coming up here to this isolated spot with a veritable stranger?

The junipers gave way to oaks and piñon. Higher, the piñon and oaks fell away, and in their place forests of Chihuahua pines reached for the frosted moon. She enjoyed the silence of the night. It was like the peaceful nights she had spent with her grandfather, long ago.

Lately she seemed to be a passionately interested observer of her own mental processes. She thought now about her marriage, and she couldn't remember any silence in it. They had always been entertaining clients and house guests, giving parties. If nothing else, there had always been the television or the radio, because Todd didn't like to be alone.

She welcomed the silence, but tonight she was desperately afraid to fall asleep. She tried talking to the man beside her. "If you're a Cheyenne, what are you doing working on a Navajo reservation, Lieutenant Watchman?"

She sensed more than saw his grin. "Staying out of the northern blizzards. I was reared in Thunder Hawk, South Dakota. Almost on the North Dakota border."

"And a career in law enforcement lured you out of the frozen north?"

He chuckled, a low, pleasant, full-bodied sound. "Hardly. As a teenager, I had so many run-ins with the local sheriff that he finally placed an extra-long cot in the cell. A baseball scholarship to New Mexico State lured me to the sunny Southwest.''

"And you majored in law enforcement?''

"Wrong. I earned a Bachelor of Arts degree in English. When I went out into the great wide world of New Mexico and Texas to seek my fortune, I learned that major oil companies don't give a hoot about Beowulf.''

For the first time in weeks she found herself smiling. A peripheral part of her mind noticed that his explanation had answered some unspoken questions that had been nagging at her. He didn't speak much, but when he did, he was fascinating. "So what did you do?''

"You might say I got desperate. After watching Inspector Erskine heroically engaging in his personal vendetta against crime on TV, I applied to the FBI. I ended up spending three arduous months in training at Quantico, Virginia. Then four freezing years in resident agencies—field offices in Anchorage, Butte, Detroit and Buffalo. Not only was I always cold, but I felt buried by asphalt and steel.''

In the dark, his laughing eyes sparkled like silver sequins. She was caught up by his wayward charm, an aura that was gentle, yet slightly reserved. "Then how did you wind up working for the BIA?''

"That's another story for another time. Close your eyes and sleep. We won't reach the cabin for another thirty minutes."

She didn't know why she followed his bidding, but her lids slid shut obligingly. When next they opened, the headlights of the BIA carryall were spotlighting a rustic log cabin with a long porch supported by cedar posts. Gingerly she eased Danny's head off her lap and got out of the car. Instantly the clean, fresh fragrance of pine trees and night-dampened grass and wild strawberries filled her head.

The nippy night air, the earthy odors, the isolation from civilization—they worked their miracle on her. It was as if all fear and agony and anger and hurt fell away. She felt rejuvenated. Up here, so close to the stars, she and Danny were safe. She stretched contentedly, as if her hands were seeking to touch those twinkling blue-hot stars. "Lovely," she murmured.

She turned to awaken Danny and found the lieutenant standing by the front fender of the carryall, staring at her. In the night, his eyes glinted like the stars. He didn't seem abashed at being caught in the act of watching her. For a moment she didn't fight his stare, because she didn't have the strength for that. Instead she yielded, letting his eyes look as deep as they dared, until he seemed to be satisfied about something.

"I'll carry your son inside," he said. "Why don't you go open the door for me? I leave it unlocked."

On the Navajo reservation she had learned that no one ever locked a door. But then, there had been little to steal. She had found so little to like about the reservation that she was a little surprised to have subconsciously headed for a childhood home she had once been eager to flee. Maybe it had been memories of her grandfather that had beckoned her. His curmudgeon's smile had held a richness that imbued her memories with warmth.

Inside, the place was dark. Behind her, Joe's low voice said, "Do you know how to light a kerosene lantern, Mrs. Richardson?"

The fine hairs on her nape were so sensitized that they were like tiny antennae, picking up the erotic signals that the man was transmitting. "Yes," she said, noting with frustration that her voice was pitched at an abnormally husky level. She cleared her throat. "Where is it?"

"On the end table to your left. Just inside the doorway. You should find a book of matches somewhere nearby."

She groped where he had indicated, and her fingers closed over the match book. She struck a light, turned up the wick, lit it, then lowered it. The lantern spread a warm sepia glow over the redwood-paneled room, making everything look as if it were trapped in a tintype. A honeyed softness glanced off a cast-iron wood stove, a leather couch polished to a high gleam by years of use, and two chairs—one a thatched-seat rocker, the other an overstuffed chair that was lumpy in spots and faded an oatmeal brown. A worn baseball mitt ornamented one antler of an eyeless elk head.

The setting was richly evocative, reminding her of a heavy quilt on a frigid winter night, providing the kind of warmth where she could fall into a deep, protected sleep.

The lieutenant, with Danny asleep in his arms, stepped around her and headed for a doorway on the far side of the room. She followed and watched him place her son on a wide bed. A thought snuck into the back of her mind. "Lieutenant Watchman," she said, "is there another bedroom?"

He straightened and stared at her, and she knew he had guessed her thoughts. "Only this one. If you're wondering where I'm going to sleep, the couch will do just fine for me. I've spent a lot of nights on it when I was too tired to pull off my boots and head for the bed. And you might as well call me Joe while you're here."

She stared up at him, wide-eyed. Collecting her thoughts, she nodded, rubbed her hands together uncertainly.

When he reached the doorway, she stepped aside to let him pass. He paused, gazing down at her, and said, "Good night, ma'am."

She blurted, "I'm grateful for all you've done, Lieutenant Watchman—Joe."

A slight smile curved the steely line of his lips, and he shoved his baseball cap to the back of his head. There was a faint line across his forehead, where the sun didn't reach. She caught a glimpse of dark, rawhide-colored hair.

"I don't think I'm finished yet."

She stiffened, alert to any possible danger in his meaning. "Come on," he said, taking her elbow. "Your lips are in a bad way."

She let him steer her into a bathroom that wasn't as big as her bedroom closet—only a shower, commode and old-fashioned sink. Above the sink, the tarnished mirror on the medicine cabinet reflected how bad she looked, as if she had just wandered in from battling a raging forest fire.

He swung back the cabinet door, and her image disappeared. "Here, this ought to do." He produced a small jar of petroleum jelly, and before she could move, captured her chin in one broad hand. The blunt forefinger of his other hand gently dabbed the petroleum jelly on her bottom lip and began to massage the ointment into her cracked skin.

In her preoccupation with caring for Danny, she had forgotten her own discomfort—the dull pain of sunburned skin and cracked lips. And she had forgotten the feel of a man's hand. Todd had never touched her this way, carefully, sweetly. Never this exquisitely sensuous touching of fingertips to lips, perhaps the most erotic parts of the body.

Wildly she wondered if his fingers had picked up on the increased tempo of her shallow breathing. An excitement she had never known stirred the almost-dead embers of her sensuous self. Could he detect the unfamiliar response of her body, welcoming his touch?

"You should have let Pamela apply her ointment to the rest of your skin," he admonished in a low, quiet voice, his fingertip tracing the bowed line of her seared upper lip.

"All I could think about was getting out of there."

When her lips moved, his finger inadvertently dabbed the salve onto her tongue. "Augh, that tastes awful!"

He chuckled, a chamois-smooth sound, and re-capped the jar. "You should at least take a tea bath for that sunburn."

Somehow she had to distract herself from his closeness. Her knees were bent on mischief. "Please ... I just want to go to sleep. I think I'm tireder than I've ever been in my life."

He closed the medicine cabinet and turned out the bathroom light. Standing there in the dark with him, she was intensely aware of the intimacy of the situation. He overwhelmed her, made an impact on her senses like the swift inhalation of a rose, or a nostalgic, heart-rending melody. Her body felt strangely fragile.

"I want to thank you," she blurted. "It seems I'm always saying that—thank you."

"Good night, ma'am."

"Please . . . call me Jaclyn."

"Good night, Jaclyn," he said, his voice whiskey-smooth.

"Good night." She slipped past him and headed for the sanctuary of the bedroom. Too exhausted to even undress, she slid beneath the bedcovers next to Danny. She had thought she would fall asleep at once, but thoughts of the Cheyenne detective wouldn't allow it. He had the power to make her feel alive in a way no other man had. And that was no simple thing to ignore. From beneath the closed door crept the dry, ticklish scent of cigarette tobacco. So, he, too, was still awake.

At last she succumbed to exhaustion and fell into a restless sleep—only to come instantly awake later, during the deep of night. She felt, rather than actually saw, the presence of someone. Between the tangle of her eyelashes, she glimpsed Joe's tall sil-

houette against the lantern-light from the outer
room. She lay absolutely still, waiting, wondering,
half-afraid that she might have misjudged him.

He placed a cool hand on her forehead. His fingers drifted down to her hand, where it lay on her
chest. They measured her shaky pulse, barely brushing her breast when he finished. He did the same to
Danny, then left the room as silently as he had come.

So, he thought, the scintillating aroma of frying
bacon had reached her.

She padded into the den on bare feet. Beneath her
brows, her eyes were sleepily sensuous. Her skirt and
blouse were rumpled, and she pushed the heavy curtain of her dark hair back from her face. It was an
unconsciously provocative gesture that emphasized
the fullness of her breasts.

"Good morning," he told her.

The smile she gave him was restless, half whimsy
and half wariness. "You wouldn't by any chance
have any coffee, would you?"

Her voice was soft. Modulated. Mesmerizing. She
was utterly different from anybody he had ever
known. She wasn't glamorous in the sense of Hol-
lywood hype. Still, he'd bet his FBI pension that
anyone around her for more than five minutes
walked away claiming she was a raving beauty. He
pulled a chipped mug, one of the better ones, out of

the cabinet, took the battered and blackened tin coffeepot off the stove, and poured her a cup.

"Thank you," she said, taking the mug between her two hands.

Her gaze, starting with his boots, rose to take in his jeans, concho belt and plaid flannel shirt. She'd probably expected him to redon the breech clout and moccasins he'd worn at the ceremonial. Idly, she crossed to the large window over the sofa, where the early-morning sunlight sifted through the streaky panes. He noticed that she was walking a little stiffly—a result of her sunburn.

"Why, the view is gorgeous! Last night I didn't realize the cabin faced the water."

"Whiskey Lake's trout fishing is right up there at the top of the charts," he said, flipping the bacon in the cast-iron skillet.

She wandered back to the kitchen and leaned against a refrigerator that rumbled like a Civil War era train engine. "Do you come up here often?"

"On the weekends, when I can get away."

"Did you build the place?"

"No. I bought it lock, stock, and barrel off an Albuquerque businessman. I left old Uncle Fred up over there—" he pointed with the fork toward the eyeless elk over the fireplace "—to remind me of the white man's need to pay tribute to his monumental ego and his needless waste."

She took a sip of the coffee. Probably drumming up a retort to his statement, he thought. She surprised him by asking instead, "How'd you hurt your fingers?"

He glanced down at the fork he held and the two crooked fingers wrapped around it. "Jammed them trying to field a grounder."

Her gaze went from his hand to his head. Shyly, she smiled over the rim of her mug. "Tell me, do you even sleep in that hat?"

He chuckled. "Only when I'm either dead tired or dead drunk."

"You don't talk much, do you?"

"To Indians, words are a white man's weapon."

She eyed him, trying to discern just how serious he was. He decided to let her make up her own mind. Meanwhile, he had a few questions of his own. "Where'd you learn desert survival?"

Her smile faded, and her lids lowered to hide whatever she was thinking. From beneath the thicket of her dense lashes, she eyed him warily. "Here and there."

"You don't talk much for a white woman, do you?"

At that the ends of her lips curled upward, reminding him that he needed to reapply salve to them. "I grew up in the high desert. At Kaibeto. My grandfather owned the trading concession there."

"Well, I'll be damned." He forked the bacon onto a platter.

"He died not too long ago."

"No mother, no father?"

"No father—or, at least, I never knew who he was. My mother was a country-western singer. No, you never heard of her," she said, responding a little tartly to the questioning look in his eyes. "She toured the small-town nightclub circuit, trying to make it to the big time. She never did. One summer I traveled with her, but it was a lonely life. I preferred to live with my grandfather, even though I hated reservation life. I always had this craving to see the world beyond the reservation, beyond the sea of red sand." She set the empty mug on the counter. "See, I do talk a lot. Too much."

Not enough. He didn't know what had prompted her to marry a man like Todd Richardson. Young love? Infatuation? Richardson's wealth? "Tell me more about Richardson and yourself."

"Like what?"

"Like how you met, for instance."

Absently, nervously, her finger circled and recircled the mug's rim. "I first met Todd when he was attending Harvard and I was nearby at Mount Holyoke College. Because we had both grown up in New Mexico... well, initially it linked us together. I was bowled over by his charm and good looks and sophistication." She glanced sidewise at him. "And, yes, I'll admit it, his background. I was too blind to see—or maybe I just didn't want to—that he glittered like fool's gold. Only after we got married did my eyes open."

He picked up her hand and lightly ran his fingertips over the back of it. He glanced up at her and caught the alarm flickering in her eyes. "You're going to peel pretty badly." Beneath his fingers, he could feel her pulse accelerate. So, she felt the same stirring he did.

"It won't be the first time," she murmured.

Like an old bear, the hair on his neck prickled. He glanced toward the bedroom doorway. The kid was standing there, those pale blue eyes glaring. The boy turned his gaze to his mother, and his eyes softened and misted over. "I thought you had left me."

At once she withdrew her hand from Joe's and crossed to her son. "Oh, Danny," she said, stooping to pull the boy into her arms, "you know I'd never, never leave you!"

"Are we still going on a vacation, Mom?"

She drew back, smoothing the hair from his eyes. "Yes, cricket. It's just that we need to rest for several days. That sunburn I got in the desert . . ."

Time to defuse the situation. Joe cracked the first of five eggs into the skillet. "I'm going fishing after breakfast, Danny. We need trout for dinner tonight. Do you know how to fly fish?"

The boy glanced at him sullenly. "No."

So, the boy's father had neglected to introduce him to the sport of fishing. "You'll learn."

Grudgingly, very grudgingly, the boy learned. Oh, Joe recognized the problem, all right. Jealousy. Danny had caught him paying attention to his mother, and the kid didn't like that. Apparently Danny Richardson had had his mother all to himself for seven years. That was unhealthy, Joe thought, and he intended to remedy the situation.

"All right, son, strip that line off the reel with your hand. Next, you whip the rod out there—pop your wrist like this. Okay, strip off six more feet and pop it again. Like you do a whip. Twitch it a time or two, so it looks like a wounded grasshopper. If nothing takes the fly, pick it up and whip it out there again."

While they fished, Jaclyn was soaking her sun-burned body in a bathtub Joe had filled with tea, and he remembered that body all too well. He could name half a dozen good reasons why he shouldn't be thinking of the woman. To begin with, according to the FBI rap sheet, she was accustomed to a high style of living: gold bracelets, Lincoln Town Cars, a vacation home on Mustique—the most exclusive private island in the world. Four years ago he had walked away from her world and its stormy quest for creative conformity.

Another reason why he shouldn't be thinking about her was sitting beside him in the boat: a kid who hated his guts. One good thing he could say about the boy, he didn't waste any breath talking. He would be the kind to learn nature's secrets quickly— if he had a mind to.

Five fish were caught, none of them by Danny, which didn't help. Joe pulled the rowboat ashore and stored the poles and tackle, while Danny trudged past him up the pine-dotted hill to the cabin. As Joe watched the flash of tennis shoes and yellow shirt until they disappeared behind the concealment of the trees, he had to wonder for the umpteenth time why he had taken on the responsibility of the woman and kid.

His field supervisor would say it was because he was a soft touch. Soft enough to let an army deserter get away. The special agent in charge hadn't been too pleased that he had let the fugitive hightail it out of Oklahoma City. The SAC had more nonessential, unimportant information at his fingertips than anyone Joe had ever met. His brain was a dustbin full of trivia. Joe grinned wryly. At least the man had known about Beowulf. He had even heard of Grendel and Grendel's mother.

Maybe it had been the army deserter who had planted the seed in Joe's mind that a regulated society left a lot to be desired. Or maybe it had been something as simple as looking at the tall, looming buildings where people lived like cliff dwellers.

So why were his thoughts centered on this Albuquerque socialite? Because her broken life fascinated him? What did that have to do with his overpowering desire to kiss her again?

Now that he knew the taste of that mouth, he wanted to taste it again—and again. His tongue tingled with the piquant sensual memory.

And his head rang with a warning. Jaclyn Richardson was not for him, could not be for him.

Chapter Five

Jaclyn wrung out the hand-washed skirt and hung it over the shower door to dry alongside her dripping blouse. This bathroom, unlike the wall-to-wall mirrored one in her condominium overlooking Albuquerque, had only the small medicine cabinet mirror. Nevertheless, she could imagine how she looked, clad in one of Joe's red flannel fishing shirts. Its hem hung past her knees, and she had had to roll the sleeves up half a dozen times to clear her wrists.

She needed clothes.

Danny needed clothes.

She needed makeup and a toothbrush and all sorts of other personal items.

What she needed was to make up her mind about what she was going to do.

She couldn't run forever. She couldn't do that to Danny. But where could she go? When could she stop running? When she ran out of places? Should she flee to Europe? Assume a new identity?

She had to make up her mind soon. Even here, Todd would find her eventually.

She ventured out into the den. Joe was cooking breakfast again, pancakes, this time. She liked watching him. His motions were clean. He was so self-sufficient; he obviously didn't need anyone. But she did. She needed Danny. He was all that was left to her to love. Anxiously, she scanned the room for him.

"He's down at the boat dock. Trying his luck at fishing."

Joe read her mind so easily. She crossed to the window. Yes, there was Danny, sitting on the dock, pole in hand. "It seems he really liked fishing yesterday. Thank you for showing him how."

Joe's gaze skimmed her length—from the freshly washed hair skewered atop her head, down past her knees, peeking out beneath the shirt, to her feet, her toenails bare of polish. "Your son hated fishing. But he's determined to beat me. I'll bet he won't return today until he has a stringer of at least six fish."

She glanced over at Joe. "Danny's not usually that antagonistic. I apologize."

"Don't." He flipped a golden-brown pancake over in the skillet. "What he's doing is making him a man."

"You speak with such authority. Do you have any children?" She joined him in the small, confining kitchen and began taking down plastic plates and glasses from a knotholed cabinet.

"No, but I do have a gaggle of younger brothers and sisters. Eight of them, three sisters and five brothers. I'm one of those middle children. The others are scattered around the United States."

Plates in hand, she passed by him, and their arms touched. Static electricity crackled along her skin. Her breath quickened and didn't let up, even as she set the dining table, one of those colonial trestle types with a pine top scrubbed clean by strong soap.

When her breathing had stabilized, she asked, "Do your parents still live on the reservation?"

He layered a pancake onto a plate stacked with others. "They're dead."

His tone was flat, forbidding further questions along that line. She asked instead, "That baseball cap—is it symbolic or something?"

An easy smile played across his mouth. "I suppose it's my way of making a statement."

Unwillingly, she responded to the enchanting up-curve of his smile. "That you march to the beat of a different tom-tom?"

He laughed. "Score one for General Custer." He glanced pointedly at her scanty clothing. "I would say you could use a wardrobe supplement. Something to get you through the next few days, anyway. I need to run into the office today. Want me to pick up some clothes for you and Danny?"

"I'd like that." She paused and felt the heated tidal wave of a blush flood her cheeks. "I need some, uhh, other items."

Beneath the cap's bill, one raven-dark brow rose questioningly. Then he nodded his understanding. "Pamela will know what all you need."

Pamela. Jaclyn pushed back unkind thoughts. To remain in this wilderness, the young nurse had to be dedicated, had to be a very caring individual, had to want to help humanity.

Or else she had to be very much in love with Lieutenant Joe Watchman.

"I'll go call Danny for breakfast," she said, using the excuse to escape her own disruptive feelings.

Barefoot, she followed a path of crunchy brown pine needles that wound between trees as straight as the teeth of a comb. Beyond, the lake glistened a pure blue in the morning sunlight. A whiptail lizard streaked from the undergrowth, and she paused to watch its ribbonlike tongue greet her.

At the end of the weather-warped dock, she stopped and called to Danny, "Hey! Breakfast!"

"I'm not hungry, Mom," he yelled back.

Even from a distance of twenty feet, she could see the determination in her son's eyes. "All right. But don't stay out all day, cricket. You'll end up getting a sunburn worse than mine," she teased.

"No chance, Mom." He pointed to the big elm behind her. "That will keep the sun off me later."

So, it appeared that her son was adapting to the wilds. When she returned to the cabin, Joe was pouring steaming coffee into cups. The pungent aroma filled the room. She slid into one of the chairs. "You're right. Danny means to stay down at the dock until he catches more fish than you did."

Joe, dissecting his stack of pancakes with all the expertise of a hunter gutting a buck, asked, "Is your son a lot like your husband?"

She wasn't caught off guard by the casualness in the lieutenant's voice. "Hardly." She poured molasses over her pancakes. "Todd is a boy who never became a man. Danny is a boy who won't rest until he does."

"Tell me about your life on the reservation."

She stared into his gray eyes. Hunter's eyes, she reminded herself. "Is this part of your standard investigating procedure, lieutenant?"

She could see that he was amused. "Consider it a personal, not a professional, question." He held her gaze patiently.

She took a fortifying swallow of her coffee. It warmed her all the way to her stomach. "I lived on the trading post for the first thirteen years of my life. For the first eight grades, I was a day student at the Kaibeto boarding school for Navajo children. I learned how it felt to be a minority problem by being one. I was shunned, never accepted into any of the play groups. The only friend I had was granddaddy."

"That bad?"

She stiffened at his tone. She didn't want his sympathy. She didn't want anything that might draw her closer to this man. Just sleeping in his bed, inhaling his scent from the pillow case, bonded her to him in a way she wouldn't have believed two short days ago.

"Not totally. I was certainly blessed to have such an unusual guardian. Granddaddy insisted that I know my prayers in Latin, double-entry bookkeeping, and how to play poker. Because of our isolation, he had the time to give me an eclectic education."

"He must have been quite a man."

"He was." Briskly, almost impersonally, she summarized those years. "One day I saw a fashion magazine blown up against a mesquite-stake corral. My mind boggled at the immensity of the world beyond the reservation, and I subscribed. Granddaddy could see how miserable I was on the reservation, so he pinched pennies and finally was able to send me east to a boarding school, Wyckenhill, in Baltimore. And after that I went to Mount Holyoke."

"Where Todd snared your heart?"

"I didn't stand a chance. We met during my freshman year, at one of those football dances, and I fell wildly in love—probably with the situation, the myth, rather than the man."

"The myth?" He had finished breakfast and was fishing in his shirt pocket for a cigarette; all the while, his eyes never left her lips.

"You know, the 'big-man-on-campus' type. Todd Richardson had already made his name at Harvard by the time he was a sophomore. Good grades, good athlete, great money, great looks. He had one of the Cozumel suntans that look as if they've been painted on—except for the tiny white streaks around his eyes. Embryonic wrinkles from smiling. He always smiled."

She didn't add that he did so because when his mouth was closed it was just a little too thin, intimating the possibility of coldness. Open, his mouth was incredible, a perfect frame for sculpted, pure-white teeth.

"I admit," she want on, "that I probably fell in love with the ideal as much as I did with the man. But, honestly, at the time, if you had asked me to distinguish between the two, I wouldn't have been able to. The two, what Todd possessed and what he actually was, seemed like the same thing to me. Still, I wasn't so blind that I didn't have doubts about our future. So did Todd's parents. After all, I was from the wrong side of the tracks. Oh, they were nice enough. Condescendingly nice. I got the message and tried to back out, but that made Todd all that much more determined to have me."

He struck a match and lit his cigarette, his eyes squinting against the smoke. "Now he doesn't want to give you up?"

"He doesn't want me to give him up," she said, not bothering to hold back her bitterness. "That would be a poor reflection on his male prowess, you see."

Joe said nothing, but she knew he was digesting what she had said. She was impressed by the intent way he listened, as well as by the quiet, forceful way he spoke. Whenever he did speak. Now, pondering her words, he rolled his cigarette around between his lips with his tongue and nipped it once or twice gently with his teeth. As she watched, she felt herself growing even more attracted to him—and she couldn't allow that.

At last he settled back to smoke his cigarette. After a moment he said, "Have you made up your mind what you want to do?"

She settled her chin on her fist and looked out at the serene lake. Sunlight was ricochetting off it, and she stared into the brightness until tears came to her eyes, because she couldn't bring herself to meet his gaze. "Start over somewhere else. Get back to the basics of life. Danny has missed out on all that. His life has been Montessori, gymnastics, trombone lessons." She slanted a rueful smile at the man across from her. "He needs to learn about doodle bugs and kites."

He rose, towering over her. "I'd suggest you wait a few more days to make a decision. Meanwhile, I'll check in at my office. I'll see what Todd Richardson is up to, then pick up some clothing for the two of you."

A little while later she watched almost with relief as his carryall spewed a rooster tail of dust as it headed down the mountain, bound for Gallup. Sexual awareness reverberated through her, and she was certain that he was aware of the unbearably exciting emotions warring within her. She couldn't help but wonder what it would be like to have a man like that

make love to her. To feel the force of his passion and
the strength of his love. He would be protective, she
knew. Gentle yet resourceful. And, she didn't doubt,
thorough.

But she doubted that he was the kind of man who
would allow himself to be shackled by the compromises required by a long-term relationship. He was
his own man. With him, a woman would know a
grand passion. A season of love. And afterward,
years of loneliness.

And yet, she would risk it, if she could be assured
of even half a chance of walking away with her
emotions unscathed. But that was an impossibility.

She cleared the dining table, washed the syrup-
and-butter-sticky dishes, then dried them and put
them away. She liked the ritual of housework. The
ordinary motions seemed to cleanse her mind of all
the pain and sorrow that her marriage to Todd had
brought her. Somewhere in those eleven years, her
sense of values had begun to dull, like a knife put to
use too many times. Being around Joe was like
walking in sunlight. He was so open. When he smiled
at her, she felt like a sunflower, compelled to forever
turn its head toward the bright sunlight.

After she finished, she strolled down to the dock.
The weather was beautiful: sunshine and blue skies
and the scent of green, growing things everywhere.
Strange, she had long ago forgotten to notice the

weather unless it annoyed her. Air conditioning and central heating took care of that.

As Danny had foreseen, the towering old elm cast its dappled shadow where he sat. "Hey, Mom, you look funny in that shirt," he said with a crooked grin.

"Thanks," she said, chuckling. She sat down next to him, letting her bare legs dangle over the rough edge of the faded redwood planks. Her toes made ripples in the cold water.

"Well," he qualified with an assessing squint, "maybe you look bad."

"Is that good?"

"Uh-huh. Ssshh, you'll scare the fish away."

She watched the sunlight hit his freckles. His T-shirt and shorts, she noticed, looked as if he had been in a mud fight and lost. "Are you having a good time?"

After a long moment he shrugged his small shoulders as if the matter was inconsequential. "Fishing's all right, I guess."

She lay back on the dock, hands behind her head, and closed her eyes. The smell of fish, sun-heated pine sap and woodsmoke from a chimney somewhere down in the valley hit her nostrils. Tranquil. She could lie there forever. She felt safe.

"Mom?" Danny yelled later. "Mom! I got one! I got a fish!"

She sprang upright, excitement quicksilvering her veins. "Well, haul it in! Quickly!"

"'Reel,' Mom!" He was rotating the handle and yanking as if a shark were fighting at the other end. "Reel it in, not haul!"

She knelt down next to him, unsure of what to do. "That's it!" she encouraged. "That's it, cricket. You almost got him. Hang in there!"

Forty-five seconds later, Danny was victorious. At that moment she would have given five years off her life to have a camera to capture his gap-toothed grin of pride, mixed with newfound self-confidence.

Then uncertainty crept into his face. "What are we going to do with the fish?"

"Did you watch Lieutenant Watchman clean the ones he caught yesterday?"

Danny's lips curled downward. He glanced away. "Not real close."

"Well, since I don't know how to clean a fish and you don't either, I'd suggest you let it go. We'll have to get Lieutenant Watchman to teach us next time."

"That's only one fish. I oughta catch some more. Just for practice."

She smiled. "Of course. For practice."

By the time she and Danny started back toward the cabin, the sun had drifted behind the trees. He hadn't eaten all day, but euphoria and triumph at catching three fish had muted his growling stomach.

Just a few days more of this idyllic retreat, she
thought, and then I'll start looking for a place for us.

All her pleasure in the day vanished at the sight of
Pamela, leaning against one of the porch's cedar
posts. The young jeans-clad nurse was watching her
and Danny make their way up the trail.

When they were close enough to hear, Pamela
said, "Hi." Her face, devoid of makeup, was both
innocent and all-wise. Jaclyn knew that behind the
mild brown eyes, the nurse's brain was assessing her
like a computer, trying to figure out what made Jaclyn tick and what threat she might offer to the status
quo of Pamela's domain.

"Hello," Jaclyn said. "Have you been here
long?"

"No. Maybe fifteen minutes. Joe and I went
shopping for you two. He got bogged down at the
BIA office on some kind of extortion case, and I told
him I'd bring your clothes on up to the cabin."

"That's kind of you. Come on inside. I'll fix you
some coffee, if you'd like."

"Oh, I know where everything is," Pamela said,
opening the screen door. "Why don't I fix the coffee while you and Danny make sure the clothes and
tennis shoes fit?" She turned to Danny with a
professional smile. "How are you feeling?" she
asked. "You don't remember me, do you?"

Wary, he shook his head.

Jaclyn laid her hand on her son's shoulder affectionately. "This is Pamela, cricket. She's a nurse. She
checked you over the night before last."

Shyly, he extended his hand to shake the one the
nurse offered and said, "Pleased to meet you."

Inside, Jaclyn took a chain-department-store bag
from the dining table and headed for the bedroom.
"What's in the bag, Mom?" Danny asked, trailing
after her.

Pamela had done well in guessing Jaclyn's size.
New jeans, stiff as starch, hugged her hips without
being too vulgar, and a peach-colored pullover
sweater was just loose enough for comfort. The tennis shoes were slightly small but, with wear, would
give a little. Along with the jeans and sweater were
several pairs of panties: all practical, all white, no
lace. A virginal granny gown and a terrycloth bath-
robe completed the ensemble.

"The jeans fit, Mom," Danny said, "but they're
too scratchy."

"We'll wash them. How about the flannel shirt?
And the socks and underwear?"

"They fit, too. Now can I take them off?" He was
anxious to get back outside.

"Sure. On your way out, why don't you look in
the kitchen for a jar of some kind. I bet you can
catch lightning bugs this evening."

He turned in the doorway, his eyes wide with curiosity. "Lightning bugs?"

She laughed. "Fireflies. I'll show you later."

She followed him out the door to find Pamela already pouring coffee into two mugs. "Thank you for shopping for me," she told the nurse. "I'm afraid I can't reimburse you right now, but—"

"Oh, you can just send a check whenever you get where you're going."

Jaclyn found the implication unmistakable. *Be on your way soon.*

"Besides, it's Joe's money." Pamela moved around the kitchen as if she were the mistress and Jaclyn her guest. "Do you take sugar or cream in your coffee, Jaclyn?"

"I'll just have it black, thank you." She sat down at the table and accepted the cup. She refused to be intimidated. She smiled perfunctorily. "How long have you known Joe?"

"Ever since I came here—three years ago. Joe had been bitten by a rabid dog—"

"Yes, I heard."

Pamela's pencil-thin brows rose in surprise. "He told you all about it?"

"Not in so many words." And that wasn't really an out-and-out lie, was it?

"Oh? Well, then you know he came to the clinic for the treatment. After that, he'd bring in a drunk with the DT's, or a kid who'd gotten in a gang fight, or a child who'd ridden his bicycle into a barbed wire fence. You never know what Joe's going to turn up with next."

She smiled at Jaclyn, and Jaclyn got the message. She and Danny were just two more of Lieutenant Joe Watchman's strays. "Just how did *you* end up on the Navajo Indian Reservation, Pamela?"

Pamela either ignored or missed the barb. "You might say that working with the less fortunate runs in my blood. My parents met in the Peace Corps. They were both stationed in Bangkok. When they returned to the United States, they settled in Phoenix. Living there, I saw both worlds: the affluent, with their countless swimming pools, and the Indians, without the very water that had once been solely theirs. I became determined that in some small way I would do something to better the Indians' world."

"That's quite commendable." Jaclyn meant it. While she had been arranging flowers and parties and attending parent-teacher conferences, Pamela had made a productive life for herself.

"I've shared my visions with Joe," Pamela said. "I want to rehabilitate the Indians. I want to bring the reservations power plants, medical clinics and industry, and then the Indian can take his place in the outside world.''

Over the rim of her mug, Jaclyn stared back at the nurse. ''I think you're making a mistake,'' she said quietly. ''Why does the Indian have to change? His is the only pure culture left.''

What had ever made Jaclyn think the nurse's eyes were mild? They were rock-hard with determination. The nurse's narrow lips pursed, but she replied calmly, patronizingly, ''We couldn't expect someone like you to understand. You see, you're a victim of your own upper-class culture. 'Affluenza,' Joe calls it. You couldn't possibly know what it's like to live like an Indian.''

Jaclyn smiled back at the nurse sweetly. ''I have a good idea.''

Pamela rose. ''Well, I really must go before it gets dark. Usually I stay over, rather than drive down the mountainside after dark.''

Jaclyn got that message, too.

At the door, Pamela paused and looked over her shoulder. In her faded face, her eyes were dark with a private anguish. ''Jaclyn, I think you should understand something. Joe is an Indian. He found out the hard way—by attempting to live in the white man's world. He's a lone wolf, a maverick. He listens to the call of the wild places. He'd never be able to return to your world without killing half of himself. I want him whole, like he is.''

She turned and left, but for a long time afterward Jaclyn stared emptily into nothingness.

Chapter Six

He took her breath away.

Muscles undulated across his broad back as he dried his hair. This was the first time Jaclyn had caught him without his baseball cap. With an inward smile, she imagined him sleeping in it. His thick hair was dark, dark as worn rawhide, and lustrous. It was cut a bit too long, she thought, perhaps hinting at the self-confident nature of the man himself.

He looped the damp towel around his neck, as thickly muscled as a prizefighter's, and strode barefoot into the kitchen, where she was making coffee. The jeans he wore followed the shape of his long legs and narrow hips. She tore her gaze away from him. Physiques like his didn't come along every day.

Only three days of brief acquaintance with the man, and she was having all sorts of wayward thoughts. Perhaps that was due to the circumstances, living intimately with a man she hardly knew. And yet she felt that she knew a great deal about him by merely being there in his cabin.

Last night he hadn't returned until late. After Pamela had left, Jaclyn had spent the rest of the afternoon and the evening alone with Danny and his flickering fireflies. Yet Joe Watchman's absence had hounded her, if only because she had been reminded constantly of him by the sight of his personal effects: a safety razor in the bathroom; a pair of muddy hunting boots lying by the front door; a badge tossed carelessly on a pinewood chest; an honest-to-goodness bow and its quiver of arrows stored in a closet.

She poured coffee into a mug and handed it to Joe. Their fingers touched, and she caught her breath. His presence did crazy things to her. "Thanks," he said. He leaned back against the counter, crossing his bare feet at the ankles, and watched her while she poured herself a cup.

He was too close; the kitchen was too confining. It seemed to have shrunk the moment he entered. She could smell the clean scent of his freshly washed skin, its coppery shade gleaming in the morning sunlight that slanted through the window. If she tried to move past him, she would have to touch him again. Could he hear the way her pulse thundered against her ears?

She avoided looking at the big man across from her, steadying her trembling hands by wrapping them around her mug while she sipped the coffee. It almost scalded her tongue. "Did you find out anything about Todd?" The subject of her ex-husband should have kept her wayward thoughts in line, but even the bleak memories of her marriage were no talisman against the powerful attraction Lieutenant Joe Watchman exerted.

"As far as I can tell," he said, "he hasn't made any further attempts to contact law enforcement authorities. Neither the FBI, the BIA, the New Mexico Highway Patrol, the sheriff's office—" he took a breath and flashed her a reassuring smile "—nor the Navajo Police have received any inquiries about you from a private citizen."

"That doesn't mean Todd's not looking for us. Probably one of his hired goons is scouring New Mexico at this very moment."

"Would he consider the possibility of your returning to your childhood home? Would he think to look for you on the Navajo Indian reservation?"

"He thinks of everything. Nothing escapes his attention. I can only hope that he and his goon will be

. . . be tempted!

**See inside for special
4 FREE BOOKS offer**

Silhouette Romance™

A FREE
Manicure Set
and Mystery Gift *await you, too!*

✂ *Clip and mail this postpaid card today! →*

Silhouette Romance™

Silhouette Books
901 Fuhrmann Blvd., P.O. Box 9013, Buffalo, NY 14240-9963

☐ **YES!** Please rush me my four Silhouette Romance novels with my FREE Manicure Set and Mystery Gift, as explained on the opposite page. I understand that I am under no obligation to purchase any books. The free books and gifts remain mine to keep.

215 CIL HAXG

NAME _____

(please print)

ADDRESS _____ APT. _____

CITY _____ STATE _____ ZIP _____

Offer limited to one per household and not valid for present subscribers. Prices subject to change.

PRINTED IN U.S.A.

SILHOUETTE "NO-RISK" GUARANTEE

Clip and mail this postpaid card today!

BUSINESS REPLY CARD

First Class · Permit No. 717 · Buffalo, NY

Postage will be paid by addressee

SILHOUETTE BOOKS
901 Fuhrmann Blvd.
P.O. Box 9013
Buffalo, N.Y. 14240-9963

NO POSTAGE
NECESSARY
IF MAILED
IN THE
UNITED STATES

satisfied by searching around Kaibeto, where I grew up."

"Maybe he's abandoned his idea of trying to take Danny away from you again."

Vehemently, she shook her head, and her hair swirled around her shoulders, tickling her neck. "You don't know Todd. He doesn't like being thwarted."

She could feel the old fear again, prickling through her veins, shaking her up. She had felt uneasy ever since Pamela's visit. The nurse viewed her as a threat. What if Pamela decided to report her presence to the authorities?

Jaclyn knew she was being irrational, but she couldn't help herself. In everything else she had always been so practical, so logical. But in this, she was terrified. She couldn't be objective about her situation. She knew only that she didn't dare trust anyone. She and Danny were together against the world. She would have to live by her wits, would have to stay one step ahead of Todd Richardson.

She put her empty mug in the sink and filled it with water. "Lieutenant Watchman—Joe—" she managed to say matter-of-factly "—could Danny and I ride with you into Gallup today? I'd like to pick up my car."

Behind her, he asked quietly, "Are you planning on running again, Jaclyn?"

She stared out the window. Soon, with autumn only a month away, the stands of aspen across the lake would look as if molten gold had been poured down the hillside. Below, on the dock, Danny sat fishing patiently.

Slowly she turned to face the big man. "No," she said honestly, "I can't do that to Danny again so soon. I just want to be prepared. I feel safe—when you're here."

"What on God's green earth makes you think you're safe with me?"

"Why, I . . ." Her voice trailed away in confusion.

His flint-gray eyes burned a path over her features: her eyes, her lips. Then they returned to claim her gaze. "We Indians are just this side of civilized," he said in a harsh voice. "Or didn't you learn that on the reservation?"

"I don't believe that's true of you." She was breathless, tingling all over under his intense regard, yet her voice was firm with certainty. "Regardless of what you say, I feel safe with you, Joe Watchman."

Exasperation played across his rugged features. His hand plowed through his hair. "I don't know which of us is the bigger fool."

"Will you?" she persisted. "Will you take us with you when you go into town?"

He pushed himself away from the counter and reached around her to set his mug in the sink. "We'll pick up your car after I make my rounds."

He was close enough for her to see his jet black pupils. Giddiness swirled through her, but she felt relief, too. That relief countered the foolishly feminine weakness she felt and gave her back her old strength of purpose. She smiled her appreciation. "Thank you. I'll get Danny."

Danny was down at the dock, still trying to beat the magical number of five fish. "Hey, Mom, look!" He held up his stringer for her to see. Already three trout thrashed about on the chain, even though the morning was still young.

"That's great. But you'll have to watch how Lieutenant Watchman cleans them this time."

He made a grimace.

"In the meantime," she continued, "we're going into town today."

"With him?" He jerked his head toward the cabin.

"Yes, with him." She was losing patience with her son. He wasn't usually so rude. No, she thought, hostile was a better description. "Now let's get going."

"Aww, Mom." But, obediently, he stored the fishing pole and followed her back to the cabin.

On the trip down the mountain with Joe, she analyzed her son's recalcitrant behavior. Danny was stubbornly silent in the back seat. Apparently he saw Joe as a threat—in much the same way, she admitted ruefully, that Pamela saw her.

On the radio a slightly nasal disk jockey was promoting the upcoming Intertribal Indian Ceremonial and playing country-western records. When a commercial came on again—"sports results brought to you courtesy of John Deere tractors" —Joe flicked the knob until he found a guttural voice speaking alternately in English and what Jaclyn thought might be Apache, since, like Navajo, it was a derivative of the Athabascan language.

She glanced over at the ruggedly handsome man beside her. He negotiated the hairpin curves that banked canyons and sheer rock faces with consummate ease. The blue baseball cap was, as always, on his head. "If you're Cheyenne, how did you learn the Navajo language?"

He grinned at her, and it was as if she had been given a view of a field full of wild marigolds. "The sink-or-swim method. I'm still far from fluent. I suppose, though, that I've mastered its intonations a great deal more easily than the average Anglo."

"My grandfather told me he lived on the reservation for seven or eight years before he began to speak the language even half decently."

"How did your grandfather end up on a reservation? Was he one of those Bible-toting missionaries?"

She smiled ruefully. "Hardly. He was an alcoholic. He came to the one place where he knew he couldn't buy a drink in a hundred miles—a reservation." For months after his death, she had felt that she might shatter if she were bumped too hard. It was still painful to talk about him unprepared. She changed the subject. "What do you have to do today?"

"Just check into the field office. See what's landed in my In basket during my absence. That's part of the perks of being a resident agent."

"A resident agent?"

"Agents who are allowed to live more or less on their own. We arrange our own lives and work with a minimum of supervision."

"Is that why you left the FBI?"

He flicked her a grin. "With some encouragement on their part. The supervisory troll in the Administrative Division felt that I was semisubversive."

"Now whatever gave him that opinion?"

"I was sent out to track down a soldier who had gone AWOL during the Viet Nam war. The man had received a Silver Star for gallantry in combat action. After ten months on the front line in the bush, watching all his buddies die, he had been sent home

on leave. He never went back. Over the next thirteen years he had made a life for himself in Oklahoma City, working as a paramedic. For two weeks
I kept him under surveillance. Observed his friends,
his wife, his three children. He was an asset to the
community, I felt. So I looked the other way while
the man fled the state with his family."

She smiled faintly. "I imagine your supervisor
wasn't too pleased about that."

"I astounded him by letting him know that the
Bureau was just a job to me, not a holy calling. After giving him that unvarnished opinion of the
profession, I thought it was wiser to resign."

"Did you really dislike it that much?"

"You might say that I was always irreverent. Un-
dermotivated. Going nowhere in particular, with little on my mind except survival."

She thought how innocent and old fashioned Joe
Watchman was in some ways. Like the desert, he was
unspoiled, unpolluted by modern civilization. He
was the polar opposite of her corrupt husband.

The Law and Order Division of the Bureau of Indian Affairs occupied a two-story brown basalt
building. Joe Watchman's office was one of several
small rooms partitioned off from the others by glass-
and-particle-board dividers. From there, secre-
taries, shift commanders and dispatchers could be
observed wandering the halls. Tacked on one wall of

his office was a Reservation map, coded with numbers.

On his desk was a stack of unfinished case files. While he flipped through the messages and radiograms in his wire In basket, Danny watched, fascinated, as a man got a drink at the water cooler. The man was dressed like a rodeo cowboy: boots, slouched hat, and a silver belt buckle the size of a saucer. On his hip he toted a .38 caliber pistol.

"Is he a BIA agent, too?" Danny asked her in a hushed voice.

"I don't know, cricket."

Joe glanced up from the pink phone message slip in his hand. "Yes. A new one. You can always tell the new ones, Danny. They walk like John Wayne. Stand in front of a mirror and pose. Parade their firearms. Everyone does it. At first I did, too. After a while, though, the role gets old."

Danny eyed him suspiciously. "You have a gun?"

Joe pulled open his desk drawer and lifted out the pistol. He broke open the bullet chamber. "See, empty. That way no one gets hurt."

Disdain curled Danny's small mouth. He turned his back on Joe and refastened his gaze on the cowboy. Jaclyn glanced apprehensively at Joe, but his expression was inscrutable. He tucked the note he held in his shirt pocket. "We've only got a couple of stops to make today."

The first stop was at Billy Baca's trading post over at Ocotillo. Buckboards, burros and battered pickups were parked in front. Inside, aisle upon aisle displayed tools, saddles, sacks of pinto beans and World War I vintage washboards. The setting was a familiar one to her, but novel to Danny. His eyes were as big as the BIA agent's belt buckle.

Behind the counter stood Billy Baca, a colorful, short and wizened Navajo who still wore his long gray hair in the old style, a *chongo*, tied in a knot at his nape. His business was flourishing due to the presence of a half dozen Anglo supervisors for the Peabody Coal Company, which was mining in the area.

"What's the problem, Billy?" Joe asked.

The Navajo couldn't have been much over five feet, and he had to strain to look up at Joe. "You know the old High Cactus mine three miles back of here?"

"The one Peabody closed down last month?"

"Yeah. Well, George Blacksheep is mad as hell about getting laid off. He's holed up inside, threatening to shoot anyone who comes near. Been there three days now. I'm afraid that crank will shoot some kid by mistake."

"You called the Navajo Tribal Police? Something like this is under Begay's jurisdiction."

"Hell, you know Begay isn't going to bother with any Indian protesting the white man's bureaucracy."

"I'll talk to George." He glanced back at her and Danny. "How about a soda pop while you wait?"

"That'll be fine," she said. Danny was busy peering through a glass-fronted counter at a gleaming assortment of buck knives.

"Give me two soda pops and two beers," Joe told Billy Baca. "And a package of cigarettes, too."

Grudgingly, the old Navajo doled out the items. "How you gonna pay?"

"Put it on my account," Joe tossed over his shoulder as he strode out the door.

Sipping from her can of soda, Jaclyn wandered around the trading post, which also served as a post office and bank, though none of its Indian patrons possessed checking accounts. She found what she was looking for—the pawn room, where Navajos traded their jewelry for credit. Turquoise and silver ornaments, tagged with the owners' names, hung on peg boards mounted on all four walls. She found a heavy silver-and-turquoise squash blossom necklace particularly lovely. The display brought back memories of her grandfather's trading post.

In less than forty-five minutes Joe was back. "George and I had a powwow, Billy. He's decided to go back home. You might want to send a sack of pinto beans over to his hogan. His wife and children could use them.''

''Who's gonna pay?''

Joe grinned amiably. ''Put it on my account.''

''Are all your BIA tasks that easy?'' she asked once they were on the road again.

''Mrs. Richardson, you've been the most difficult one.'' Beneath the shadow of his cap, the half smile he slanted her softened his words.

''Where to now?''

''The last stop. The Red Rock State Park east of Gallup. This afternoon is the beginning of the annual Intertribal Indian Ceremonial. I just want to check it out and make sure that the visitors are orderly. The Navajo Tribal Police will be on duty there full-time. We sort of work in conjunction with each other.''

''I remember going to two or three ceremonials with my grandfather. They reminded me of the fairs where my mother sang.''

What Jaclyn hadn't remembered was how crowded the ceremonials could be. They were a three-day weekend for the whole family. In this male-dominated society, the women walked behind their husbands. Youngsters ran everywhere. Teenage girls shyly flirted with even shyer teenage boys. Old women gossiped, and old men enjoyed the chance to get together and share a bottle of the ubiquitous *tis-*

win, corn whiskey made in stills hidden deep in the canyons.

Danny found the Indians fascinating. A rodeo clown juggling gourd rattles attracted his particular interest. Then he watched the Navajo shepherdesses in their bright velveteen blouses and gathered skirts. One buck paraded by in a breech clout with a Stetson and sunglasses. Another sported sandals and a large silver cross over a crimson velour shirt.

"His people would say he has left the Navajo Way for the Jesus Road," Joe told Danny, who stared, open-mouthed.

Next Danny was enthralled by the dancers, who wore eagle masks of papier mâché that covered their entire heads. While one man pounded a drum, the dozen or so dancers circled and swooped, their feather-bedecked arms outstretched, the bells on their moccasins tinkling.

Afterward she and Danny strolled through the parade grounds with Joe. There was so much to distract the eye: the indoor and outdoor marketplaces; a rodeo; games; demonstrations in the small plazas; and even more exhibitions of Indian dances. On a streamer-draped stage young women competed for the Miss Intertribal title.

Occasionally Joe would stop and chat pleasantly with an acquaintance. Jaclyn noticed, though, that beneath the billed cap, his eyes were constantly scanning the crowd, assessing potentially disruptive situations.

She also noticed that the dusky Indian maidens didn't miss a chance to cast flirtatious glances in his direction. And why not? There was no missing him. He was taller than anyone else there, and built better than Samson, not to mention the powerfully masculine cast of his features.

The superb craftwork of the Zuni, Navajo and Pueblo tribes filled the shops and outdoor stalls: rugs, jewelry, pottery, kachina dolls and baskets. The Indians went deliberately about the serious business of buying and selling. Some squatted in the shade of a stall, others gathered by their pickups in sociable groups to make conversation.

"Joe!" a little girl's voice called.

Off to Joe's left, Jaclyn glimpsed Gracie, with her sister Tessa in hand. Both girls wore grins as wide as jack-o'-lanterns.

"*Ya-ta-hey*, Gracie, Tessa," Joe said easily, hunkering down so he was at their eye level. The two girls positively beamed. Gracie wrapped her arms around his muscled neck in a delighted hug. Tessa put her tiny hands to her mouth and giggled. Her coal-black eyes left Joe, to fasten on Danny, and more giggles peeled from her rosebud mouth. Danny's mouth slid into an abashed, lopsided smile.

"Where's your grandmother?" Joe asked.

Gracie pointed behind her. Not far away Old Martha sat on a low stool beside a blanket spread with her wares—pillows, folded rugs and saddle blankets.

"Let's go see if Old Martha Two Goats got her burros and buckboard back in good condition," Joe said to Jaclyn.

He grasped her elbow, guiding her across the crowded fairground. His mere touch made her reckless with a primal longing. Almost shyly, she remembered the way he had kissed her—forcefully and, paradoxically, tenderly. She was discovering secrets of human passion that she had never known, discovering her own latent sensuality. The revelations filled her heart with both excitement and curiosity.

When they reached the Navajo grandmother, the old woman grinned, flashing her silver front tooth, and rattled off something in the Navajo tongue to Joe. He chuckled and made a reply, then glanced down at Jaclyn. "Martha wanted to know if I'd like to buy a marriage blanket for you."

"What did you tell her?"

The amusement remained in his voice, but his eyes darkened noticeably. "That you're not looking for a husband."

And he wasn't looking for a wife. She lowered her gaze, unable to meet his quicksilver one. "Did she say if Mona and Lisa brought the wagon back all right?"

He translated her question, and Old Martha Two Goats grinned again, and said, "Yabetcha!"

While he talked with Old Martha, Jaclyn browsed through the blankets and rugs the Navajo woman had woven. The textiles were bright with intense colors. The quality of the workmanship was excellent. Jaclyn had learned how to discern quality work from her grandfather, who fervently believed that Navajo rugs deserved the same respect and status as that enjoyed by the Persian rugs.

"How much?" she asked Martha, holding up a rug that had caught her interest, one with almost fluorescent red-and-white flowers.

"Thirty dollars." The old woman winked. "For you, twenty-five."

Jaclyn didn't have more than three dollars or she would have bought it. Martha was selling the rugs far too cheaply. Too late, after the Navajo woman was dead, her work would be recognized for its brilliance.

"Joe, please tell her that I will return one day to buy a dozen from her." She winked back at Old Martha. With the Navajo grandmother, Jaclyn didn't feel so much like an outsider. "Tell her that's a promise."

Gracie and Tessa wanted Danny, who they seemed to have adopted, to stay with them and watch the parade, which was starting in half an hour, at dusk. Jaclyn was reluctant to let him out of her sight, even for just an hour or so. She knew she was being paranoid, that her son had to lead a normal life, that old Martha would watch him as carefully as she did her granddaughters. And if Jaclyn didn't know all that, she saw the reassurance clearly in Joe's eyes, and so she relented.

The stalls were beginning to cast the long shadows of evening on the fairgrounds, and Joe stopped at a food stand to buy corn dogs. "It seems that I'm running up quite a tab on your generosity," she told him, taking the corn dog he passed her.

He grinned down at her. "Oh, I plan on collecting." His statement caught her off guard, but not as much as the next moment, when he passed a calloused fingertip over the distended fullness of her lips. The touch of his finger was an inadvertent caress, marking her skin with its warmth and softness, igniting her senses. The gesture was in no way made less intimate when he explained, "You had mustard on your mouth."

When they paused to watch what the white man termed a squaw dance, one Indian maiden singled Joe out and tried to drag him by the belt into the circle of dancers, where the women clung to the backs of the men's belts.

Joe smiled, but shook his head no, saying something in Navajo to the pretty young woman.

"What did you tell her?" Jaclyn asked, her curiosity piqued.

He smiled down at her. "That I was on duty."

Stars were already twinkling in a sky still faint with sunlight when Joe stopped by the Chapter House, a large brick building tucked into a grove of cottonwoods near the end of the fairground. Inside the brightly lit lobby, where a teenage boy was taking tickets, Joe pointed to the upper walls. Near the ceiling a stylized depiction of a woman ran along the perimeter of the room, her feet beginning above one side of the entryway and her head ending above the other side.

"The Rainbow Maiden," he said.

Jaclyn knew vaguely of the *Yei* figure. "A guardian spirit, isn't she?"

"Yes. The Rainbow Maiden covers the walls and thus protects the building." His grin was gently mocking. "Note her square head. If you remember your Navajo art, you'll recall that all females have square heads, while males are portrayed with round ones."

Jaclyn's smile carved dimples beneath her full cheekbones. "Don't get cocky, lieutenant. That's because women are more levelheaded."

His eyes communicated his delight with her. "I would hate to have you as an opponent in a debate."

The Chapter House was designated for a variety of uses—from political rallies to rug auctions to dances. In fact, a dance was in progress in the main room. A country-western tune blared from a wooden stage assembled at the front. A banner tacked above the stage proclaimed *Dine Bizel*—Navajo Power. Dancers circled the sawdust-covered floor in a thirty-five-mile-an-hour Texas Twostep.

In the dim light Jaclyn saw Indians dressed in every possible type of garb, from blue jeans and long flounced skirts to Bermuda shorts and miniskirts. Then she glimpsed Pamela among the dancers. The nurse was with a rather nice-looking middle-aged man in a khaki shirt and trousers. Apparently Pamela had also seen them, because when the dance ended she and her partner came over. She greeted both Joe and Jaclyn, but her hungry gaze clung to Joe.

"Marshall," he said, shaking her partner's outstretched hand, "I haven't seen you in a while."

The man flashed a pleasant smile. "The Agency is keeping me busy."

"This is Marshall Lawrence, the director of the BIA's Western Navajo Agency in Tuba City," Joe said to Jaclyn, and she knew he had purposely avoided giving the man her name. The decision was up to her.

"You look familiar," Marshall said, a puzzled frown etching his suntanned face. "Have we met before?"

Immediately, she placed him. The year before she had gone east to boarding school, Marshall had often visited her grandfather's trading post whenever matters at the Kaibeto school required him to make the fifty-mile trip from Tuba City headquarters. He was a genuinely nice man, but she couldn't risk his recognizing her.

"I don't think so." Abruptly, she turned to Joe. "I like this song. Could we dance?"

For a frozen moment she thought he would tell *her*, too, that he was on duty. But then she saw the understanding in his eyes. He nodded and propelled her into the crowd of dancers. Shackled in his arms, she felt safe—and something else. Light . . . alive . . . reckless. His body was solid and delicious. And very, very male.

She dared a quick glance up at his dark face. Those hunter's eyes were watching her with a stern purpose. The social smile on her lips died. His arm tightened, drawing her against him.

Foolish! Foolish! But she thought she would faint with the force of the sensations ravishing her body. For thirty years she had lain concealed like a cactus flower in the sand, waiting for that preordained moment when it would burst out and enrich the desert with its dazzling perfection.

And now...now, too late, she was unfolding the petals of her inner self for this man. An Indian. A member of the people who had made her childhood a time of loneliness, of unhappiness. A man who could never live in her world any more than she could live in his.

Chapter Seven

The knife blade glinted silver in the sunlight. From the porch swing, Jaclyn watched Joe Watchman clean the trout on the dock below. Danny sat beside him, apparently engrossed in fishing, but she was willing to bet that he was watching Joe, too, albeit covertly. More than likely that was why Joe was cleaning the fish that afternoon—so that her son would have an opportunity to see how it was done without actually being instructed.

When he finished, Joe dropped the last fish in a pail of water with the others. He was shirtless, and the turquoise water reflected sunlight off his broad back. She felt merciless desire grab at her throat. Pail in hand, he started up the hill toward the cabin. She had only a glimpse of the coppery expanse of his chest before he became a part of the woods. A few minutes later he emerged from the towering pines. She knew he was aware of her, sitting in the swing, but she also knew that until he had something to say, he wouldn't waste words on empty speech.

After setting the pail on the edge of the porch, he strode over to a barrel, placed under the cedar eaves to collect rain water. He washed his hands and splashed the water over his face. Watching him, her whole body prickled. Water droplets sparkled at his throat and on his chest. He was too tempting, nice and clean and golden in the slanting sunlight.

He joined her on the porch, and the swing creaked beneath his weight, but held firm. Their glances locked, the exchange eloquent, laced with an elemental understanding. He draped his arm across the back of the swing, not quite touching her.

He wants to touch me, she realized. But he never made the move she knew he longed to.

"I like it here in the mountains," she said to ease the ache of longing inside her. "Everything is so fresh that you can even smell the green. I feel pure here."

"And did you feel impure before?"

The swing swayed gently back and forth. After a moment of introspection, she answered honestly,

"Yes. As Todd's wife, I helped him entertain, helped him conclude deals made at a dinner party, during a game of mixed doubles, or over lunch at the country club. Gradually my eyes were opened to his bag of tricks—the way he manipulated people, his ruthlessness, his shady dealings. Nothing outright illegal, you understand. Always in the gray areas. Because I said nothing, I became a partner in his deceptions. A member of his Clod Squad, as I call them."

"Clod Squad?"

"Men in dapper pin-stripe suits who scurried around to carry out his bidding. Yes-men. Goons."

Joe smiled. That smile gave her no peace. It was a smile that said he knew her very well—and planned to know her better. "You've kept this pain, this guilt, like a stone in your stomach. Very unwise."

He was probing too deeply, and her glance slid away from his. "Perhaps, but the pain, the guilt, anything was better than the sterility of my life."

"Leave it behind you, as you are leaving him behind you." His fingers brushed aside the damp wisps of hair clinging to her brow. He stared, sightlessly, at his hand for a moment before seeking her gaze.

His expression shook her. Every cell of her was alive to him. She sat rosy-cheeked and breathless. She needed him to take her mouth in a long, melting kiss and ease this intense, hungry aching.

"Joe," she murmured.

He stopped her with a light pressure of his hand on her mouth. His palm was a caress, igniting her senses, leaving her mouth tingling and unbearably excited. "The white man talks too much."

As he watched, she managed a smile, trying to overcome the mist of yearning in her eyes. She would never know what might have happened next, because he went suddenly still, then looked out toward the lake. She knew his finely sensitized hearing was picking up something she couldn't catch yet. Following his gaze, she saw a plume of dust drifting along the shoreline.

She glanced back at him. He rose, motioning for her to remain where she was, and strode down the graveled drive, past her Lincoln and his carryall, to await their visitor. The pulse in her throat throbbed. Every moment held a terrible feeling of anticipation. Despite the heat of the afternoon, she felt sticky and cold. Light perspiration gathered between her breasts. She was tempted to run down the tree-blanketed hill and gather Danny safely to her side, but she knew she would have to trust in Joe to protect them both.

She heard the car drive up, heard another man's voice, then saw Joe and another man coming around the side of the cabin. She tensed. The other man was Marshall. She sat back in the swing, waiting. Joe wouldn't have let Marshall approach her if he thought the man was a threat. Still, she felt uncertain.

Marshall propped his crossed arms on the balustrade in front of the swing. Above a scattering of freckles, his eyes were teasing—and kind. "I remember who you are now. Jaclyn Dobson. The last time I saw you, you had pigtails and knobby knees."

Warily, her gaze sought out Joe, his big shoulder braced against one of the upright cedar posts, his gray eyes watching them both. "It's all right. I explained the circumstances of your being here."

Her breath zephyred out between her trembling lips. She leaned forward and touched Marshall's arm. "I'm sorry. I was so afraid of losing Danny that I couldn't trust anyone."

He grinned. "You trusted Joe here. I'm an older friend than he is."

She glanced at Joe. His eyes were shuttered. She smiled back at Marshall. "Ahh, but Joe was there when I needed him." She had injected a bantering note into her voice, but what she said was the truth. "How did you know where to find me?"

"I pressured Pamela until she finally gave up and told me you were hiding out up here at Joe's cabin. I swear my lips are sealed."

Danny was walking out from beneath the trees, and somehow, in the midst of introductions, Marshall wound up getting invited to stay for a fish fry. In the end she was grateful for his presence. It reduced the sweet tension that was building between her and Joe.

While Joe fried the trout, Marshall peeled potatoes, and she made a salad, brewed tea and set the table. Camaraderie filled the small kitchen, as crowded and hot as it was. "I'll open a window," she said.

The kitchen window was stuck. Before she knew it, Joe came up behind her, braced his hands on the sash on either side of hers and raised it easily. For several seconds their stance was almost an embrace. She could feel his hard body pressed behind her. She gasped for air.

When they moved apart she tried not to let her eyes linger on him and betray her tumultuous feelings to the perceptive Marshall. The evening air, with the scent of meadow grass and water, filtering through to cool the cabin, restored her facade of serenity.

If Marshall noticed anything out of the ordinary, he didn't let on. Instead he kidded her about the time when he caught her trying to smoke behind the trading post. "I distinctly remember that you reeked of smoke, and your face had a sickly green look."

She laughed, remembering the event. "Three Navajo girls had dared me. They were always taunting me, and I had learned that if I showed weakness, they wouldn't let up. I certainly couldn't let them call me a coward, could I?"

Danny, who was sitting in the rocking chair, was all ears. He was grinning with delight at this new side of his mother. "Danny, why don't you try to catch fireflies again? We can use their light to eat by tonight."

"Aww, Mom, you just don't want me to hear you talking about when you were a kid."

She forced a smile to her lips, because he was absolutely right. There were other stories of her childhood that weren't so amusing. "Never mind, young man, you go round up some fireflies."

With another, "Aww, Mom," he collected his jar and was off. Several times she saw his shadow darting after beckoning, intermittent flashes of yellow.

At last dinner was ready, but somehow the camaraderie had evaporated, despite the enchanting light cast by the jar of fireflies sitting in the center of the table. While Marshall charmed Danny with delightful tales of reservation life—a side that she had failed to witness—Joe smoked and listened, saying little. She realized then that Joe's silence was one of the more practical forms of aggression.

Apparently Marshall realized it, too, because he took his leave early, even though Joe invited him to spend the night. "I really shouldn't. I need to get an early start tomorrow. Tuba City's a long way off."

After he left, Danny freed the fireflies, then tumbled into bed, tired from an active day. As she listened to his sleepy prayer, she could hear Joe in the outer room, clearing away the dishes. With Danny tucked in, she shut the bedroom door and went into the kitchen.

The lantern cast a gleaming circle of golden light. In such close quarters with the big Cheyenne, she felt diminutive, feminine and, yes, even timid. She had never thought of herself as timid, yet in his presence she grew tremulous. "Let me help," she said.

His smile was broad. "Lady, I won't argue with that offer."

The consoling warmth of the dishwater made working beside Joe Watchman easier. Still, her throat was arid, her face tense. They were so close that she could have reached up and removed his baseball cap, could have run her fingers through the burnished brown of his hair.

He worked alongside her, drying while she washed. The silence was raw. She felt tongue-tied. After several minutes he spoke. "You talk easily with Marshall. Are you afraid of me?" he asked softly.

She hesitated.

"You weren't afraid of me when you were defending your son out there in the desert."

Eyes forward, hands usefully employed, she said, "That was different. I feel...uncertain around you."

Embarrassed, she stole a quick glance up at him. His expression seemed to indicate that he had hoped she would look at him. She watched, enchanted, as the corners of his mouth curved upward. "Why? Because I'm an Indian?"

"No...because...well, I'm not sure why."

His gray eyes were warm, his body relaxed, almost lazy, as he leaned his hips against the counter and dried a cup. "It was difficult for you, living with the Navajo, wasn't it?"

She nodded. It wasn't easy talking about her childhood, but it was easier than admitting the feelings for him that were causing such chaotic commotion inside her. She spoke slowly, carefully choosing her words. "Very difficult. Sometimes the Indian children made fun of me. Or spat at me. I felt ugly around them. Their skins were the shade of the beautiful sandstone formations, while mine was colorless. I hated being an outsider, and I couldn't wait to grow up and leave. But I felt pulled apart, because I didn't want to leave Granddaddy."

"And now you've come back," he said quietly.

A flutter stole along her nerves as his hand reached out to push back a heavy lock of the hair clinging damply to her neck. Slowly his fingers skimmed lower, just inside her sweater's deep vee neckline. His fingertips glided lazily, following the line of her neck to her collarbone, where her pulse beat erratically in the hollow of her throat.

Because of her isolated childhood, she had been frightfully shy in her college years and had dated only one man, Todd Richardson. Now Joe Watchman was turning her inside out. She could feel the color building in her cheeks. When his fingers lingered on her skin, she whispered sadly, "But I won't be staying."

He lifted his other hand, and the delicate pressure of his fingertips grazed one nipple, stroking her through the soft fabric of her sweater. "I know you won't. I also know I like touching you, Jaclyn. But I'm afraid I couldn't stop at just touching." She watched a gentleness creep into his eyes. "Go to bed. I'll finish up here."

She retreated, though all her emotions clamored for her to remain.

The tufted leather couch was miserably uncomfortable. Joe's legs extended well beyond the end. Finally he stretched out on the floor. It wasn't the same as sleeping on the ground. The feeling of being part of the earth when you slept on it, night after night, was an enormous experience. A connection was formed—intimate and consoling—of a man and the land.

He regretted getting out of that habit. Now it looked like he ought to think about renewing it. At least until Jaclyn and the kid left.

The kid. The kid hated the sight of him. Those "dead" blue eyes spat venom, as poisonous as a Gila monster. Yet Joe couldn't help but like the kid. Danny had determination. He was going to make it in life despite his father.

Joe thought about his own father. How he had loved him. How his father and mother had destroyed each other. Literally.

A switch in his mind clicked off, and he called forth another image. That of Jaclyn Richardson. Half naked, a part of his desert. A fierce lioness protecting her cub. Her charming laughter at the rodeo clown. Her laughter remained with him like the whispered fragrance of a sachet.

But getting involved with a woman like her would mean changing his way of life. Why shouldn't he? Why live like this, sweating during the days and freezing during the nights? Why not work only five days a week? Why not work nine to five in an air-conditioned office? Why not own a half dozen suits and an economy car and earn two weeks vacation every year?

Because he couldn't. He simply couldn't.

For four years now he had avoided the horrors of that life, and he wasn't about to start seeking it out now.

Angry at the direction his thoughts were taking, he rolled restlessly onto his back, hands behind his head. He usually slept in the buff. For the sake of propriety he had slept in briefs the last few nights. He didn't even have to return to the cabin every night. He could have slept at his Gallup apartment.

So why did he make the hour and a half trip up into the hills instead? Because she had told him she felt safer when he was there.

Oh, come on, Joe Watchman! he taunted himself. You never were one for lying to yourself. You make the trip because you want to see her again. See her every night.

Soon she would be leaving. Then he could return to his apartment, as plain and empty of life as this cabin was full of it—now that she was here.

The night air had an edge of cold to it. The cold seeped through the plank floor, chilling his bare torso, chilling even his thinking. He ignored the discomfort, seeing it as a way of keeping his mind off *her*.

Outside, the black sky momentarily turned bright with lightning. The Wind People rattled at the windows. The moon hung halfway up in the sky, the yellow of its rising gone and its face turned to ice. It

was an autumn moon. Clouds scarred its visage.
Thunderclouds. The thunder rolled across the heavens, vibrating the cabin.

At once he stilled. He was as inanimate as the furniture, merely a part of the room's contents. Faint sounds reached his finely tuned hearing. Then he identified them. They were nightmare sounds. He had made them himself as a lost child, even as a rebellious teenager. And then as an iconoclastic young man. Now he no longer knew how to cry.

Rolling to his feet, he lit the kerosene lamp on the end table, then padded soundlessly across the plank floor to the bedroom. Easing open the door, he stood for a moment, his gaze piercing the night to find his bed. Danny lay there in the deep sleep that came from an active day.

She was asleep, too, but her hands made little knotting movements. Her head moved restlessly. Curled up, she looked frail, sweet.

He knelt beside the bed, careful not to waken her suddenly. Instead he gentled her. Smoothing sweat-dampened hair from her cheek. Stroking her brow. Whispering soothing words in her ear. Cheyenne words of endearment that came naturally to his tongue. Words he hoped she wouldn't understand.

The lulling words reached her subconscious. Her tightly clenched fists uncurled. Her rapid breathing slowed. Her breasts, barely constrained by the vir-

ginal white cotton nightgown, ceased their agitated
rise and fall. The grim set of her mouth eased. Her
alabaster neck was shadowed by a scattering of
drifting midnight curls. He had never been drawn to
blondes. Dark-haired women were, to him, mysterious and complex.

If he leaned a few inches closer, he could stir those
curls with his breath.

He couldn't help himself. He lowered his mouth
over her parted lips. Sweet. Soft. They responded to
the movements of his own. Their mouths became
one. He was breathing her scent, tasting her sweet-
ness. If only for that moment, she was his Guine-
vere, his Isolde, his Beatrice.

Where was the self-discipline every Indian learned
as a child? With a monumental effort he regained
control of himself and lifted his head. Against the
night shadows of her hair, her skin was a pale bisque,
her lips the color of a tea rose.

She sighed languidly. He knew when her eyes
opened. Her lashes quivered and slowly lifted,
brushing the side of his thumb. "I was having a bad
dream," she murmured.

"Yes."

She buried her face against his chest. Her lashes,
damp with unshed tears, feathered across his skin.
"Oh, Joe, it was awful!" Her words were smoth-

ered. "Todd. He was chasing us. I was trying to run, but I couldn't. Danny was so heavy in my arms."

"Ssshh. It's all right." There he was, using that phrase to comfort her again. Next to her, Danny stirred, disturbed in his sleep.

Joe gathered her up into his arms and carried her from the bedroom into the den. He sat down in the thatched-seated rocker, with her cradled in his lap, and began to rock. Her breath was warm against the hollow of his throat. The soft lamplight picked up the pastel shade of her complexion. Sable curls wreathed her pale cheeks, and her unpainted toe-nails peeked from beneath the hem of her gown.

Outside, lightning flashed. She burrowed deeper within his arms. Her hair, a cloud of midnight against his lips, clung damply to her shoulders, spreading in a shimmering web.

He was comforted by the knowledge that she would be leaving soon. In a matter of a week or so she would be gone. That meant his self-control need not last forever. In the meantime, his feelings were too rich to restrain.

"Joe?" she said sleepily. Her hair glowed in the lamplight like moon shadows.

"Yes?"

"Why haven't you ever gotten married?"

He didn't want to lie to her. So he answered instead, "I reckoned there was no way any woman could domesticate me into a house cat."

Her head made a slight negative motion, and her hair tickled his chin. He glanced down to catch a faint smile tugging at her lips.

"Some detective you are. You don't know anything about women, Lieutenant Joe Watchman."

"Hey, I'm a damned good detective. Everyone at the Detroit agency said so. When another agent needed to track down a criminal, he'd ask me to put my ear to the pavement. Sure enough, I'd—"

Her laughter bubbled through her lips. "You're incorrigible!" She snuggled closer against him. "Now, Tall Chief, tell me more of your exploits."

He talked of a few, invented others merely for her entertainment. Talked and rocked. At last she went to sleep, and he rose and carried her to her bed. When he returned to his place on the den floor, he couldn't sleep. He was like an old dog, rolling this way and that, getting up, pacing in circles.

His head was too full of her. He felt as if he might never sleep again.

Chapter Eight

She supposed she was becoming obsessed with Joe Watchman. Lieutenant Joe Watchman. His rugged good looks were only incidental to her need for him.

She imagined he was working late. Or maybe he wasn't coming at all. When he had told her that she and Danny could put up at the cabin, he hadn't promised her that he would stay there with her to comfort her, as he had the night before. She had just assumed he would always be there when she needed him. And that was something she had no right to believe.

Soon she would be leaving. She could never stay on the reservation, not only because of the childhood experiences that had left scars on her heart, but also because of Danny. She didn't want him to be treated as an outsider, as she had been. She could never subject him to the loneliness and rejection she had known.

Yet, just as it had broken her heart to leave her grandfather, so it would break her heart to leave Joe. But he belonged to another world; he had turned his back on her world.

That night she made dinner for herself and Danny, slicing and frying a canned ham she had found in the well-stocked pantry. Sitting across the table from her, her son chewed noisily on his food. She had to smile. He looked so healthy, such a different boy from the tense child she had taken from Todd's condominium in Houston. His face was tanned, his solid little body almost pulsating with vigor and sunshine.

After dinner they played gin rummy with a deck of dog-eared cards she had noticed in a catch-all drawer earlier. Joe's cards?

Danny's mouth crimped in a triumphant grin. "All I need is one more card to gin!"

"I bet I know what card you need. Is it a three of diamonds?"

"Mom, you cheated!"

She laughed. "I didn't. I guessed."

Four hands later, at ten o'clock, they put the deck away and turned in. Danny barely got his "amen" out before his lids slid closed. She lay beside him, unable to sleep. At first she was too hot, so she rose to open the window. The night air shivered with a bird song. Momentarily contented, she arched her back, pressing her hands against the hollow of her spine. But her contentment ebbed, and she crept back into bed. She rolled onto her back, flipped onto her stomach, then turned back over again. Without Joe near, she felt strangely restless.

Much later she heard the low purr of a car engine. She wasn't certain of the time, but the moon had already traversed the width of her window. Her earlier apprehension that Todd would find her and Danny at the cabin returned to nag at her. She lay strung as taut as a bow in the bed. The car drove up to the cabin and parked. Perspiration beaded on her upper lip. Her ears strained to hear footsteps. When she heard a porch board groan, she scrambled out of the bed and went to the bedroom door, listening.

An unearthly silence followed, and her voice cracked as she called softly, "Joe?"

"Yes, it's me. Go on back to bed."

Sweet relief rushed through her like a spring flood through a desert wash. She sagged against the door. All was right with the world.

Once more she returned to bed and lay there, listening to Joe move about in the outer room. His step was so light that several moments would pass before she heard another footfall, and then it was only the slightest of sounds. About half an hour later she heard the front door creak open, then shut, but she didn't hear the carryall start up again. What was he doing?

A playful breeze full of the last fragrance of summer wafted through the window, beckoning. The night murmured, inviting her outside. Clad only in her nightgown, she gave in to nature's enticements. The wooden floor of the front room was cool beneath her feet. Uncertain, she stood at the screen door and stared out. The sky was filled with brilliant stars over a horizon made jagged by the silhouettes of the trees. The meadow grass smelled sweet.

Then her eyes found Joe, his mighty frame picked out by the starlight. He appeared to be gazing out at the lake. After a moment he hunkered down on one knee with that unhurried grace peculiar to him and lit a cigarette.

What was he thinking as he smoked it?

His powerful sixth sense must have warned him of an intruder watching, because he turned his head toward the porch door. There was no way he could see her, because she was still inside the darkened room, yet he called quietly, "Come out and join me."

She heeded his call, and the damp grass tickled her toes. Then she dropped down beside him and sat upright, hugging her tucked legs, her cheek resting on one of her knees. "I'm sorry," she began. She combed her fingers through the grass. The earth had a rich, licheny scent. "I didn't want to disturb you."

He flipped his cigarette out into the night and settled back, his elbows propped behind him, his body comfortably stretched. "You didn't. How's Danny? Did he clean his fish today?"

"No, he threw the five he caught back in the lake."

He laughed softly. "It won't be long before he surpasses me."

And when he does, it will be time for us to go, she thought sadly.

"He saw your bow in the closet today. I told him it was for hunting deer."

"Do you know anything about hunting deer?"

She smiled to herself. "Not about hunting them, exactly. But Granddaddy used to talk about them."

"What did he say?"

"Oh, that deer are like Indians. That they can smell for miles. But that they don't smell so well if the wind is blowing strong, or if it's raining. He told me they have a great sense of hearing. That they can actually hear you breathing." She could feel Joe's eyes on her, but she couldn't look at him. Whenever she did, her heart refused to stay in tempo with the rest of her body's natural rhythms.

"Your grandfather sounds to me like a man who loved nature."

"He did. We used to sit out under the summer sky and watch for shooting stars. I missed seeing them when I went east. Too many city lights on the horizon, he told me. His face seemed so beautiful to me, Joe. Wonderful and alive, like a kachina doll. I used to love to touch his hair. It was white and wild, but soft and fine. Angel hair."

In the darkness, Joe's eyes were as silver as the stars. His passion came through in his voice; he was hiding nothing. "I like touching *your* hair, Jaclyn. I like touching *you*."

With an unswerving, wide-eyed gaze, she watched as he leaned toward her. Stars drifted down around them. His fingertips lifted her chin, and his lips ruffled soft kisses along her cheekbone before making a long, sensitive journey down to her mouth. Cool and soft, their lips moved against each other. His tongue touched the inside of her mouth, and she heard the rapid patter of her heart and felt her skin grow hot. Without conscious volition, her hands splayed against his shoulders, so solid, so hard.

He tilted her chin higher, deepening his access to her sweet mouth until she could only hold on to him tightly, experiencing over and over again the exquisite sensation of his kiss. She shivered under the sweet stroking of his tongue. It filled her mouth, delving deeper with ever harder strokes.

His hands moved around her back, drawing her closer. She wanted him. Wanted to be under him. To feel the goodness of him.

He sensed what she wanted; how could he avoid it, when he wanted the same thing? They began to caress each other through their clothes, their hands desperately seeking. He lifted her breast, cupping its fullness with gentle pressure. The surface of her skin burned, and inside she was shudderingly warm.

Her lips sought his smooth chest. She inhaled deeply of him, wanting to absorb all of him into her. He smelled of sweet grass and cool summer breezes. She murmured incoherent words against him, all the while feathering feverish kisses across his skin, where it sheathed the strength of muscle and bone.

He lifted his head and stared down at her face with passion-tormented eyes. The deep silence of the night was broken by his erratic breathing. "This is crazy, Jaclyn."

"No," she breathed, "it's the only thing in the world that's sane."

"Don't you see," he asked with great tenderness, "that if I make love to you, I'll want to do it again and again? Danny already hates me. You don't want him to hate you, too. And what happens, Jaclyn, when you leave? Should I make it a hundred times harder for us by—"

She stopped him with the shaky pressure of her fingers against his mouth. "I know. I know," she said sadly.

Jaclyn dared only to glance at Joe the next morning; she couldn't bring herself to meet his direct gaze. She was bewildered by the feelings that unknown horizons were taking hold of her, wild and inevitable. She was torn. She wanted to stay with him. She wanted to flee with Danny. She wanted to run again, because she had run out of ways to make sense out of anything.

Joe set his empty coffee mug on the counter. His smile was inviting, his eyes even more so. "I need to drop by the Crown Point rug auction this afternoon. Would you and Danny like to come along? Old Martha Two Goats's granddaughters will be there. I think he would enjoy being with children his own age, if only for a few hours."

The mention of Danny's name put Jaclyn's worries back into perspective. She couldn't panic and run every time a threatening situation arose. For Danny's sake, she had to achieve some semblance of normality and stability in their lives. She owed Danny a few more days respite, at least.

Was she thinking only of Danny? Or, if she was honest with herself, didn't she also want to buy herself a few more days of these new feelings, this new passionate self, that she was discovering?

She wouldn't consider that now. She would simply do what she longed to do and go with Joe. "We'd like that very much."

Crown Point, Jaclyn discovered, was a small, remote town in the midst of black and brick-red stone escarpments. The auction was being held at the Crown Point Elementary School. Although it was only six o'clock, buyers were already there to view the offerings in order to prepare their bids.

As if they had radar, Gracie and Tessa honed in on Joe immediately, squealing with delight as he pitched first one, then the other, into the air. And if Danny thought he could keep safe by hiding behind Jaclyn, the girls quickly proved him wrong. They grabbed his hands and tugged him along with them. Pigtails swinging, Gracie said to Jaclyn, "We're going to the playground, all right?"

"An attendant will watch them," Joe said.

"Sure," Jaclyn said, smiling.

Joe, his hand at the small of her back, directed her through the press of people, some of whom had come from as far away as Albuquerque and Flagstaff for the auction. "People travel so far because of the mystique," Joe explained. "I think they like to see the women in their native costumes. But the serious collectors come because the Crown Point auctions have a reputation as a source of quality merchandise. The collectors either buy here, or privately, from a trader or a weaver who they know.''

The large gymnasium, smelling slightly of tennis shoes and sweat, was already filling up with bidders taking seats in the folding chairs provided. Joe found Old Martha behind the gym, in what was the locker room, with several other Navajo women. She was registering her weavings with an officious-looking, balding man seated behind a desk. Jaclyn was once again impressed by the quality of Old Martha's work.

The Navajo woman flashed her a knowing grin. ''Uh-huh, you two need marriage blanket.''

Jaclyn could feel another blush suffusing her skin. She couldn't think of a thing to say.

Joe took pity and rescued Jaclyn. ''I need to take a look around the grounds, make sure everything is in order. Would you be interested in staying here and watching the bidding?''

''Very much.''

He led her back to the gym and found her a seat. The auction had already begun. Beneath a basketball hoop, a spindly man wearing jeans, a western hat and a checked shirt was directing the bidding from a dais improvised from wooden crates. He told stories laced with humor about each rug, in effect giving its "pedigree." It took four to five minutes to sell each piece.

When one of Old Martha Two Goats's rugs came up he said, "Hey, looky here, folks. This is one of them political rugs." His teenage daughter, the assistant, displayed both sides. "See? Two-faced. Let's start the bidding on number 106. Do I hear fifty dollars? Come on, folks. What the heck? It's only money."

When no one signaled a bid, Jaclyn took a risk and bid fifty dollars that she didn't possess. At least, not at the moment. That started things, with others raising the amount, and she felt a little easier. Within three minutes the bidding was over.

"Number 106 sold at one twenty-five!" called the auctioneer. "Next, now here's a jim-dandy saddle blanket..."

One hundred and twenty-five dollars! A rug of that size and quality shouldn't have been sold for less than a thousand. She thought of the work that went into something like that. Weaving a single rug sometimes took years.

Suddenly disgusted, she rose from her chair and edged through the people standing in the doorway. She went to find Joe.

A dimly lit hallway led past the locker room. At the end of the hall, lights from the playground spilled through the double doors. She stepped out onto the porch and stood for a moment in the shadows, watching the children play. Danny, grinning happily, was pushing a roundabout filled with half a dozen laughing girls and boys.

"He's going to be all right, Jaclyn."

Startled, she whirled to find Joe, one hand braced against the brick wall, watching her. His smile was tender, and as charming as an old-fashioned photo.

She swallowed and tried to smile. She felt both shy and nervous. She had felt that way ever since last night, when he had kissed her.

As she gazed up at him now, urgency's hard, bright notes sang in her blood.

He leaned toward her and lowered his head to hers. Foolish, she thought, to get giddy every time he drew near her, but she couldn't help herself. He caressed her neck.

"You tempt me so much, lady," he muttered before his lips met hers.

She was in love with this gentle man, she realized in the moment before she surrendered to the domination of his kiss. She opened her mouth to his tongue, hard and demanding and conquering. His body leaned into hers, pressing her against the wall that still held the heat of the afternoon sun, just as his body held the heat of his need for her. She felt his knee between her thighs, and her body became exquisitely weak. She held on to his iron-ridged shoulders for support, her hips and breasts seeking the powerful feel of him.

For just those few magical moments she would believe that there were only the two of them in the world. That she would never have to return to civilization with Danny.

But reality was too strong. As Joe released her she heard Gracie and Tessa calling to him. She looked past him and saw the girls skipping toward him, with Danny trailing behind. All three of them were breathless from exercise.

"Why don't you go inside and get a drink from the fountain?" she suggested to them.

After the children scampered off, she turned to Joe, placed her hand on his arm and said, "Please, could you help me talk to Old Martha? I have something I'd like to tell her."

He glanced down at her hand, and she felt her heart flutter against her ribcage. He took her hand and pressed it against his heart. Her fingertips picked up the powerful thudding. "See what you do to me," he said quietly.

Later, while she tried to explain her idea to Old Martha—her grandfather's idea, really—Jaclyn still felt lightheaded from Joe's melting kisses, his strong hands stroking over her skin.

"Joe, tell her that she and the other weavers need to form an association. They need to achieve economic independence. They should start marketing their own work."

The three of them were standing just outside the gym, in a quiet corner of the hallway. Old Martha cocked her head, listening intently as Joe translated.

"What I'd like to suggest," Jaclyn said, "is that Old Martha and some of the other weavers contact a bank, which can provide the backing for such a venture."

When Joe finished translating, Old Martha bobbed her head enthusiastically. She grinned at Jaclyn, her black eyes glistening in her leathery face. "Yabetcha."

She extended her gnarled hand, and Jaclyn shook it warmly. She owed the old Navajo woman a debt for helping them to recover from their near-fatal exposure to the desert sun.

As she was shaking Old Martha's hand, a flash-bulb exploded. She glanced over to see two men in casual business dress—jackets with no ties. Both carried cameras, but one was busy jotting notes. Their press badges identified them as being from the *Albuquerque Journal*. She had noticed the pair earlier. They had been taking photos of the bidding, the children and the women in their brilliant-colored costumes.

The one who had just taken the photo was getting ready to snap another when Joe stepped between her and the photographer.

"I'm with the BIA Law and Order Division. I'll have to take that film. Cameras are prohibited during Navajo activities."

The photographer glowered at Joe. "Crown Point isn't reservation land by a good ten miles."

"That may be, but this is an Indian activity, and no photos are permitted. May I have the film?"

The words emerged as a demand rather than a request, and Joe's impressive build combined with his tone to persuade the man to hand over his film, however ungraciously.

After the newspapermen had departed in a huff, Jaclyn said, "Joe, Old Martha could have used that publicity."

His eyes narrowed. "Yes, but you couldn't."

Chapter Nine

Joe looked like a sleeping giant as he lay on the floor, his head pillowed on an arm striated with muscles. The overpowering maleness of him ignited Jaclyn like a blow torch. Even asleep, he exuded assurance and willfulness. He was so self-sufficient, so arrogantly virile. Desire swept through her with the force of a flood, and, like the desert when the rains came, she was unprepared for it.

Weak-kneed, she sank into a chair across from where he lay, the same chair where he had rocked her. She let her eyes feast on his magnificence: the proud curve of his cheekbones; his overwhelming strength; the barely veiled danger he could present;

his sensitivity. She thought, too, what a dark romantic he was. How had he ever survived the cold, mechanical impersonality of city life?

A wry smile found its way to her lips. He wasn't wearing his baseball cap.

She remembered being cradled in his arms the night before last, recalled the way he had stroked her temples and cared for her when she was in the throes of her nightmare. And she recalled his searing kisses. Suddenly, her breasts were full and painful with wanting him. She felt an urge to kneel beside him, to run her hands adoringly over his body. She craved the taste and smell of him.

Abruptly she rose to her feet and crossed to the front door, silently opening it so as not to awaken either him or Danny. She had to flee the cabin and the passion that waited there to claim her.

"Where are you going?"

She spun in her tracks, her hand on the doorknob. His seemingly lazy-lidded eyes were watching her. "I—I thought you were asleep."

"I was. Until I heard you get out of bed."

Then he must know she had been staring at him like a spinster at the town's newest bachelor. She felt the heat rise in her cheeks. "Why didn't you say something?"

"I just did."

"You know. Before."

"I didn't want to disturb whatever it was you were thinking."

She hoped that he didn't have a clue as to what her thoughts had been. Something, however, whispered that he did. Mortified, she could not let the revealing conversation continue.

"I was going swimming," she blurted.

"At seven-fifteen in the morning?"

She managed a nonchalant shrug. "Why not?"

His lambent eyes slid over her jeans and sweater. One arrow-straight brow slanted in a questioning angle at her attire, but he said only, "Why not, indeed? I think I'll join you."

She couldn't comment on the fact he was wearing only his briefs without exposing her own clothes to comment, so she said nothing as they walked together down the secluded path that led to the lake. The morning chill laced the air, and the leaves glistened from the light rain that had fallen during the night.

She could think of absolutely nothing to say, and he, as usual, felt no compulsion to say anything. He was confident and controlled, and she vowed that she, too, would say nothing. She wouldn't babble, wouldn't drink her own rain of words.

When they reached the dock she paused, then turned to face him. His mouth was curved in a smile, warm, but with an edge of intention. His smile announced that he wanted her badly, and that she was about to have to deal with that fact.

She knew that he had intentionally positioned her so that, in order to look up into his face, she had to squint into the rising sun. "I don't usually undress in front of strangers," she told him breathlessly.

"I undressed you before this." With each word, he stepped closer.

She took a step backward, trying to escape his coaxing presence. "That was...that was different."

Deep laughter rose from his chest. "All right. I'll let you off the hook." With that he dove cleanly into the mirror-smooth water, briefs and all.

Quickly, she stepped out of her jeans, then flung off her sweater. Clad in her panties and bra, she dove off the opposite side of the dock. The chilly water snatched her breath.

So did the sight of Joe, who was only three feet away when she surfaced. Water droplets spiked his thick lashes and glistened on his coppery skin, weathered by the high-country sun. At the look of dark purpose in his eyes, she felt as if she had been invaded by electric currents. She treaded water, waiting for she knew not what, as he swam nearer.

His hand pushed back the wet strands of hair that clung to her face. His flint-gray eyes burned a path over her features one by one: her eyes, her lips, her brow. He bent his head to breathe damp kisses along her hairline and near her ear.

"I know I have no right to say this," he said, his voice deepened even further by the raw ache in it. "But, God help me, I want you. I've been wanting you for a long time now."

Her hand splayed across his chest, warm and velvety smooth. Beneath her fingertips, his heartbeat altered, accelerated, became a steady, heavy thudding. She felt the tension in the muscles of his chest, felt the uneasy contraction of the skin over his ribcage.

"Joe, love me . . . please love me."

"I've been doing that from the first day I found you. Didn't you know?"

"Yes." The word came as a single breath. But she knew that in his love, unlike hers, there could be nothing that would last. No permanency.

He captured her hand, holding it gently, and drew her against his length. She found herself supported against his broad chest as he lay back and floated in the water. Each time he moved, he drew a sensual response from her. In the green depths beneath them, his legs made a cradle against hers, suspending them in a netherworld.

Her arms slid around his neck, and her lids fluttered closed. When his lips, cool and wet, claimed hers, she felt a sweet singing in her blood. His arm slipped around her supportively, even as his tongue entered her mouth to take possession.

She shuddered uncontrollably at the deliciously erotic feelings that coursed through her, short-circuiting her usually analytical thought processes. In that instant she discovered a passion that had waited, hidden, in her until this moment. Heat spread in her, curling almost painfully in her stomach.

When she opened her eyes, he was gazing down at her with such passion that she was rendered helpless with bewildering desire. Her breasts strained painfully against her bra, seeking the warmth of his flesh, and a sensation she couldn't interpret shivered through her.

Her words were breathless. "You do strange things to me, Joe Watchman. Teach me how to do them to you."

His gaze rapt, he said, "You already are." Then he kissed her soft, swollen mouth again.

Locked together, they kissed until their breath came in hard, shock-filled gasps. They kissed in lost ways. Incoherent, guileless words, half sentences, elated phrases sang between them.

When at last he raised his head, she was too joy-filled to say anything. Unable to help herself, she traced the steely line of his lips with one fingertip.

"I'll give you a year to stop that," he said, grinning wickedly.

A flush of love heat flared in her. Her body seemed unbound by the law of gravity. She wanted to tell him that she loved him, but shyness—and futility— numbed her tongue.

Suddenly his gaze lifted, fastening on something slightly beyond her. She glanced over her shoulder. Danny was walking onto the dock, pole in hand. Immediately she started to pull away, and Joe said, "No. Danny has to understand that it's all right for you to be attracted to a man. We'll return to the dock together."

But Danny was already stalking away.

Jaclyn wrung out her wet hair, which was draped over one shoulder, and water droplets hit the shower's tile floor. She had risen early, careful not to awaken Danny. He had slept restlessly the night before. She could only hope that the silent hurt she had seen in his eyes all day yesterday would be erased by sleep. Did he feel that she had betrayed him and his father by falling in love with Joe Watchman?

It was a foolish question. Danny couldn't know that she was in love. Or was it true that children could sense things beyond the range of the average adult?

There were no more clean towels in the bathroom cabinet, and she reached for one Joe had used earlier that morning. He had left before sunrise to do a follow-up on a grocery store robbery in Window

Rock. She had lain in bed, straining to hear his quiet movements, as he showered and dressed. Only when she knew he had gone did she get up.

She felt a little self-conscious as she brought the fluffy towel to her face and nuzzled it, inhaling deeply. There was nothing artificial, no cologne, only the redolence of fresh air and sunshine and Joe's own masculine scent. The darkness that had been hounding her for years seemed to recede.

She put on her robe and opened the bathroom door to find Joe just entering the cabin. Slowly, without taking his eyes off her, he shut the door behind him. The sight of him sent tiny, eerie sparks dancing along her nerves. She felt shaky inside. Even the air seemed different. Sensation rose in her chest, an undeniable response to his masculinity. She could feel her perceptions narrowing until she was aware of only him. The towel she held dangled uselessly from her hand.

She took one step toward him, and it was like stepping into a dream. He took the towel from her lax fingers and dropped it at their feet. "I thought you had gone," she murmured.

"I came back for my cap." The way he looked at her made her heart tumble.

As she gazed into the pagan glitter of his eyes, she reached up to winnow her fingers through his thick hair. Its scent reached her, reminding her of the fragrance of pleasure. He caught her hand and brought it to his lips.

"So soft," he muttered.

He released her hand then and gently laid his own on her waist beneath the robe, curving his palm to her bare flesh. The back of his other hand rubbed comfortingly, lightly, along her cheek. She turned her head slightly to press her lips against his hand, to feel the texture of his firm, clean-scented skin.

"Kiss me, Joe Watchman," she whispered.

It seemed to her that the air crackled around them. He took a deep breath. "I don't know if I can stop at just kissing you. Where you're concerned, my self-control has been obliterated."

She slid her hands up over his shoulders, feeling the delicious warmth of him. He shuddered; then his arms came around her. He buried his hand in her damp hair and gently tugged her head back, tilting her mouth to his. At first his kiss was softer than dawn's first tenuous rays drifting through the window. His chest was firm against her breasts, and his hips pressed against hers with sweet strength. His hands roamed over her hot, love-ready flesh, and she gasped as he covered her belly with slow, erotic strokes. Then he lifted one of her breasts, his fingers gently kneading, and she trembled with the force of her passion.

With a shaky breath, he set her away from him, his eyes hot with emotion. "I want you so badly. I'm tempted to carry you out into the forest right now. To take you there on the earth, just as I found you. But I can't.'' He smiled wryly. ''For so many reasons, I can't.''

Despair filled Jaclyn's heart, driving away the warmth she had felt only moments before. She knew his reasons—knew them all too clearly. Joe could never be domesticated, never become a house cat, just as she could never change her spots and become a desert animal.

A phrase leaped from the back of her mind: *And never the twain shall meet.*

Reluctantly, she stepped back and watched him leave the cabin.

A week. A full week that she and Danny had spent at the isolated fishing cabin. How easily she and her son had adapted to Joe Watchman's life-style. In these pastoral surroundings, she had come to feel clean, new. Gone was her cynicism. She had shed all the anxiety and pain that had clung to her when she was the wife of a petty man, unable to care for others. Whatever substance had run in Todd Richardson's blood, the milk of human kindness was conspicuous by its absence.

The sweet tension of living together was building between her and Joe. As she cleaned up that morning, she thought about how grateful she was for whatever time the Lord chose to allot them.

If only Danny could be more willing to accept Joe. Perhaps that would somehow change things and leave her free to follow her heart. She had planned on speaking to her son after Joe left. He was to be gone only a couple of hours, enough time for her to really talk with Danny. But Danny, upon awakening, had magically reverted to the loving child he had been before, leaving her no opening for serious conversation.

"Mom?"

"Hmm?"

He gave her a hug. "Come fishing with me, Mom."

"As soon as I clear the breakfast table." She set the cups in the sink. "Have you learned how to clean your fish yet?"

His eyes went cold. "I didn't need to. I just let them go."

"Mmm. All right. I'll be down soon." She swatted his backside. "Go on with you, fisherman."

She never made it down to the dock. A visitor arrived a few minutes later—Pamela. Jaclyn watched the nurse swing down easily from the cab of her pickup, which she had parked next to Jaclyn's Lincoln.

Pamela, Jaclyn thought, *was* Joe's type of woman. She was so capable, so independent. She didn't need anyone the way Jaclyn did. In the early morning sunlight Pamela looked vibrant. Her long hair,

clasped at her nape, was as yellow as the petals of a
black-eyed Susan, and her eyes were as dark as its
center.

Jaclyn greeted the other woman at the door with
a social smile of the sort she had always reserved for
Todd's business associates. "Good morning, Pamela. What brings you up this way?"

"I had a patient to call on down in the lower valley. Just thought I'd stop by and chat."

I bet. The nurse hadn't driven this far out of the
way just to chat. She must have seen Joe in town and
known that Jaclyn would be alone.

Jaclyn motioned to the redwood swing on the
porch. "Let's sit outside. It's so nice this early in the
morning. I'll put on another pot of coffee."

"No, no. That's all right. I won't be staying long."
Pamela sat at one end of the swing and stared pointedly at Jaclyn. "Will you?"

"Will I be staying long?" Jaclyn repeated. She was
still standing at the door. A slow anger began to
simmer inside her. She crossed to the porch railing
opposite the swing and braced her hips against the
rough cedar bark, staring hard at the young woman
across from her. "I'll stay as long as I need to. And
as long as Joe will have us."

Pamela lifted a sun-bleached brow. "That's aw-
fully risky, isn't it?"

"I don't know what you're talking about."

"Do you really think this living arrangement is best for your son?"

"That's my business."

"Then think about what's best for Joe."

Jaclyn barely disguised the impatience rising in her like black bile. "And I suppose you know what that is?"

Pamela bit her lip and looked away from Jaclyn's unwavering gaze. "That's why I came by. I'm concerned for him."

Jaclyn clenched her teeth so tightly that she thought her fillings would fuse together. "Please get to the point."

"The point is that you have the power to hurt him. If you only understood him...understood his past..."

"Why don't you explain, then?"

Pamela rose and wandered over to the front steps. She leaned against the opposite side of the post, making it difficult for Jaclyn to view her face. But her voice held a depthless sorrow that Jaclyn couldn't miss.

"Joe's father was one of those high-rise construction workers. You've heard of them—the Indians who are famous for balancing on girders swaying thousands of feet above the ground. Fearless men. Joe's father worked in places like Chicago and New York, but Joe's mother was never happy in the concrete cities. Her husband wasn't either, for that matter. He was an alcoholic. One day he came home and shot his wife, then turned the rifle on himself."

Jaclyn found her hands gripping the railing on which she sat, her fingers digging into the rough wood. She drew a steadying breath. "That's a tragic story. But I fail to see the analogy."

Pamela turned and fixed her with diamond-hard eyes. "If you lure Joe back to the big cities..." She swallowed hard, then said grimly, "Like his father, Joe has a dark side."

Jaclyn's brow wrinkled. "I don't understand. Are you trying to warn me. Are you concerned for our safety? Is that it?"

"No!" The nurse's skin was stretched tautly over her narrow face. "I couldn't care less about you or your son. Your kind always survives. I'm concerned for Joe. And if you love him even half as much as I do, you'll be concerned, too!"

This time Jaclyn couldn't pretend not to understand. And the knowledge of what she would have to do left an emptiness inside her, a hollow that hurt more than she had ever thought possible.

Chapter Ten

With trembling fingers, Jaclyn tucked her blouse into the waistband of her skirt. At the same time she wriggled a foot into one of her alligator shoes.

Where was the other one?

And she still had Danny's clothing to collect. Joe could return at any moment. There was so little time!

She could have sworn she had put both shoes in the bedroom closet. She dropped to her knees and looked under the bed. Her blood congealed. A leather rifle case. She swallowed hard, scrambling to her feet. Where was the blasted shoe? Precious seconds were ticking by. She shoved the swath of hair that had fallen forward out of her face.

That was it! The bathroom. Yes, there it was, behind the door. Her gaze swept the rest of the bathroom, then the bedroom. Was she forgetting anything? With only one shoe on, the other still in hand, she hobbled to the closet. The hangers slid along the metal bar like beads on an abacus. She dumped Danny's old clothes into the bag in which Pamela had brought their new ones.

"Are you running again?"

She spun around. Joe was standing in the doorway. He was relaxed, his legs slightly apart, his hands on his hips. He closed the door behind him, his expression as unreadable as a Navajo sand painting.

She tried a smile, a tremulous one. "Just like an Indian—to sneak up on someone like that."

"I asked you if you were running again?" His inflection never altered.

She avoided his eyes. "Yes."

"Why now?"

She occupied herself by sliding her foot into her other shoe. Act calm, controlled, confident, she commanded herself. "Sooner or later Todd will track us down. We've been here too long as it is. We've overstayed your hospitality." She slid her purse strap over her shoulder. "I've been thinking about Danny." She fumbled in her purse for her car keys. "The sooner we get permanently settled somewhere, the better."

She looked up to find Joe standing directly in front of her. He pushed the baseball cap back on his head and stared down at her, his eyes searching her face, as if committing her features to memory. There was no way he could miss the pain trembling on her lips, stiffening her posture so she wouldn't shake. The way he looked at her made her body go haywire. Her blood danced in her veins. Her skin tingled. Her ears buzzed.

Dear God, she loved him so! Her emotions were no longer segregated into orderly areas, some cerebral, some physical. She wanted Joe Watchman with her body, wanted him with her mind, wanted him with her entire being. But if she loved him, truly loved him . . . Pamela was right.

"What's happened? Tell me."

"Nothing. You've been very kind, Joe. We appreciate all you've—"

"Cut it out, Jaclyn." His mouth tightened and he stepped back. "Pamela was here at the cabin. I saw her tire tracks alongside your Lincoln. What did she say to you to scare you off?"

"We just talked." She stepped around him. "I ought to call Danny. He needs to get ready."

She got as far as the front door, then stopped. Her hand froze on the knob, and she pressed her forehead against the door. After a moment she said, "Pamela told me about your parents. About your father killing your mother and himself."

He came up behind her, bracing his hands on either side of her. He was so close to her, so big, so virile. "So that's it. You're afraid that one day I'll repeat my father's actions. Then you should know the whole truth."

If a voice could be steaming with anger, she thought, Joe's was. "Please, that's not it at all, and I don't want to hear any more," she begged, heartsick.

He ignored her. "It seems my father came home one afternoon and found my mother in bed with another man." His lips twisted sardonically. "He kicked the man out of the bed, shot him, then shot my mother. Then he got in bed with her and shot himself."

She shuddered and spun to look up into his eyes. They were darker now, the color of smoke from a forest fire. "My God, how terrible for you."

"Actually," he said, his voice casual, but unable to hide his pain, "I was too young—six or seven—to realize the horror of the situation at the time. I was sent back to the reservation to live with one of my older brothers and his wife." He smiled grimly. "Does that satisfy your damn curiosity?"

Inside, her tears fell, fracturing her into fragments, but she wouldn't allow them to show. "Yes."

His big hand closed over her shoulders and moved her away from the door.

"Where are you going?" she asked.

He stared down at her. All the tenderness he had once shown her was absent from his features. "Back to Gallup."

She listened to him drive away. I won't box you in, Joe Watchman, she vowed silently. I won't force you to become a white man.

With her heart crumbling, she made her way down to the dock. Danny saw her coming and waved. When she got close he said, his eyes dancing, "There's a humongous fish out there, and I'm gonna catch him today, Mom."

"We're leaving, Danny."

"Leaving?" She couldn't tell whether he was pleased or disappointed. "Where are we going?"

She wasn't certain. She knew only that they were going where there would be no desert to remind her of Joe. "Maybe Vancouver." The rain forests of Washington state would be a far cry from the desert—and yet the city was small enough for Danny to continue to discover the pleasures of boyhood.

"Does Vancouver have plastic worms?"

In spite of the heaviness of her heart, she smiled. "I'm sure it does."

"Are there any lakes near there?"

"A big river—and not far from that an entire ocean. The Pacific. Now put the rod away. I've already packed our clothes."

* * *

Driving along Interstate 40, Jaclyn reflected on her last-minute decision to go out of her way to travel back east to Albuquerque first. She was taking an awful risk. The police could still be watching for her car. But she had a debt she wanted to repay: to Old Martha Two Goats. This would be her love gift to Joe. Later, when he learned about it, she knew that he, and only he, would be able to understand and fully appreciate what she had done.

Reaching Albuquerque reminded her that in the short space of less than two weeks she had grown out of tune with cities: the highways that didn't seem to take you anywhere; the metallic taste of the hazy air; the constant noise; the hurry-hurry-hurry attitude of the people. She realized now that the glamour of a big city was only a synthetic excitement.

The American Indian National Bank's Albuquerque field office was located in the Indian Pueblo Cultural Center, modeled after Pueblo Bonito in Chaco Canyon, the biggest and most advanced of the ancient Southwestern cities, inhabited over 1,200 years before.

The account representative was an attractive man wearing a seersucker sports jacket and sporting long, blue-ribboned black braids. "Jim Namingha," he said, introducing himself.

A telephone call interrupted him, and she overheard a discussion of liens and loans with, presumably, a Pueblo potter. Danny, bored and antsy, sat in an overstuffed chair, swinging his feet. When Mr. Namingha got back to them, he was affable and listened politely to her proposal: arranging a loan for Old Martha. With the bank's backing, a collaborative project such as the one Jaclyn envisioned for the Crown Point rug weavers could become a reality.

When she had finished speaking, Namingha folded his hands on his chest and rocked in his chair for a long half minute. At last he said, "I like your idea of a coalition of Navajo weavers. But you must understand that meeting the needs of 252 Indian communities located in 26 states requires more than a mere financial consideration of a prospective client. Still, I believe in your project. I'll need financial statements and collateral. Talk to some of the women about this enterprise. Tell them to come in next week and we'll begin filling out the necessary forms."

Perhaps God did work miracles and didn't leave everything to nature, she thought. "They'll be in," she said in a firm tone.

She omitted that she would inform Old Martha only by way of a letter or a telephone call to Marshall. Or even Pamela. The young nurse might not trust her, but Pamela sincerely wanted to help the Indians. As far as the matter of collateral went, Jaclyn knew Joe would never accept any money she might send to repay him. Her repayment would be sent as collateral for the loan.

After Namingha arranged for her to cash a check, she and Danny left. Satisfied with all that she had accomplished, she managed to chat with Danny and feign a lightheartedness she was far from feeling on the drive back along I-40. This would be her last time to pass through the high desert country. As they drove through Gallup, Danny complained of being thirsty, and reluctantly she began to look for a place to stop. She thought nervously that there was a chance Joe would be in town and spot her car.

She stopped outside a store with a burnt out neon sign proclaiming, Tokay Wine Sold Here, then plunked down a dollar for two cold drinks. As she waited for her change, her glance skimmed the racks of the latest editions of the Window Rock, Gallup and Albuquerque newspapers. She almost didn't notice the photo on the front page of the *Albuquerque Journal*.

Almost.

Her blood turned icy. The photo was a close-up of Old Martha and herself, shaking hands. The caption below read: "Old Martha Two Goats, a Navajo rug weaver, concludes a deal with a new client at the semimonthly Crown Point Rug Auction."

Mechanically, her hands trembling, Jaclyn picked up and paid for the newspaper. She folded it up, then glanced at her Lincoln. Danny was sitting inside, placidly chomping on a piece of bubble gum.

Her legs as limp as licorice sticks, she hurried back to the car, saying nothing to Danny as she handed him his cold drink can. She backed out of the parking lot, then drove quickly onto I-40. Maybe the scent of her fear had attracted Todd, she thought a few minutes later, because when she glanced in her rearview mirror, a light blue Chevelle appeared to be following two cars behind. Despair iced her spine.

Accelerating, she immediately exited onto old Highway 66, heading north. The Chevelle stayed with her, gaining on her. Now only one car separated them. She took an exit marked Mexican Springs. The road turned out to be unpaved. Her sweaty hands gripped the steering wheel as she tried to keep control of the car, which rocketed over the washboard road. She glanced in the mirror again, and when she didn't see the Chevelle, hope blossomed in her chest. Then, as the dust her car churned up settled, her hope wilted. The Chevelle was right behind her.

Danny sensed her panic. "What's wrong, Mom? Why are you driving so fast?"

What could she say? That his father was going to take him away from her again? Danny didn't understand—and shouldn't have to cope with—that kind of a situation. "I'm just in a hurry."

Trustingly, he didn't question her.

Mexican Springs was a collection of abandoned hogans falling to ruin in the shadows of a black escarpment. Ahead, the road simply ended. Tears of frustration filled her eyes.

"No," she muttered, brushing angrily at her damp cheeks.

Quickly she killed the engine and unbuckled her seat belt. "Danny, we're being followed! You're going to need to run very fast. Can you?"

He grinned, excited by what seemed like an adventure to him. "Like a jackrabbit!"

Keeping him in front of her, she started along a path that meandered up the escarpment. She stopped to glance back at the village below. The figure getting out of the blue car was unmistakable.

Todd!

She turned back, keeping her gaze on Danny's small shoulders. She would not look around again. The path grew tortuous, a series of seeming cul de sacs, and cruelly steep. Once she paused to take off her heels, discarding them where they lay. Even Danny was slowing down.

The hot air scorched her windpipe and lungs. At the start of the climb she had been breathing through her nose. After fifteen minutes, the demands of the climb became too great, and she began to breathe through her mouth. Within minutes her tongue felt thick, and her lungs wheezed like collapsed bellows.

Danny was beginning to drag. "Mom," he croaked, "I'm . . . tired."

She stopped, her breath coming in agonized gasps. Making a supreme effort, she picked up her son and hugged his little body close to her. If God was listening...

Joe glanced up from a case file folder he was reviewing. Pamela was in the outer office, striding purposefully toward his cubicle. As soon as she entered his office, she shut the door behind her; her face was tense.

"That bad, eh?" he asked.

"Worse." She handed him the newspaper.

Jaclyn's profile, along with Old Martha's, was captured in a photograph, front page. Joe cursed silently, eloquently. The other photographer. He must have snapped a photo, too.

Joe rose from behind his desk. "I'm going up to the cabin."

"She's not there. I already checked this afternoon, as soon as I saw the newspaper. I was going to warn her."

He wasn't surprised that Jaclyn wasn't at the cabin. Hadn't he known from the start that she wouldn't be staying permanently? "You're a kind woman, Pamela."

"No, I'm not." Her mouth leveled in a nononsense line. "If I didn't love you so much, if I didn't want the best for you, Joe, I would have reported her to someone a long time ago."

Almost from the start, he had made it clear to Pamela that he wasn't interested in her as more than a friend. Now he understood fully what the pain of loving someone and being unable to have that person meant. His gaze strayed to his office window. A formidable-looking thunderhead was building over the distant mesas, and a matching sadness built in him. He had hoped to win Jaclyn and Danny, and now he had the heart-wrenching feeling that he would never readjust to life without them.

Pamela was saying, "About an hour ago, a man stopped by the clinic with this picture. He wanted to know if I had seen her and a little boy in the past ten days. That's when I decided you had better know about the photo immediately."

Fear, a feeling he had thought he would never know again, sliced through him. Fear for Jaclyn and Danny. "I'd bet my FBI pension it's Jaclyn's ex-husband," he muttered.

"So that's what this is all about. He wants her and the boy back?"

"He wants *her* back. The boy is just a means to an end. Did you see what kind of car he was driving?"

She grinned. "I think I've been around you too long, Joe Watchman. I told him he might check with the Window Rock police, and went outside to show him how to get to the police station." She dug into her pocket and pulled out a folded slip of paper.

"His license plate number. He's driving a late model Chevelle. Baby blue."

"Good girl!" He picked up the telephone and dialed the in-house radio dispatcher. "Put out a local for a baby-blue Chevelle bearing the L.P...." He paused, then read out the number.

"Don't have to, Joe." The dispatcher's voice was scratchy. "Hofstetler spotted a Chevelle headed north on 66 out of Gallup, maybe ten minutes ago. Following a Lincoln. Both doing in excess of 80."

"Did Hofstetler give chase?"

"Nah. You know our deputy sheriff. Not one to put himself out. As soon as the two cars turned off onto Mexican Springs road and made it onto reservation land, he radioed the report to us and dumped them."

"Get a hold of Hofstetler. Tell him I'm on my way to Mexican Springs."

"I'm coming with you," Pamela said. "And you can't stop me."

He grinned, even though he didn't feel like it. His guts were a twisted knot of death-dealing rage directed at Richardson—and at himself, for not being more careful. He should have demanded the film from both cameras, but, somehow, kissing Jaclyn mere minutes before the incident had shaken his reasoning processes. "Never thought I could stop you, Pamela. Let's go."

Once they were out of Gallup, he drove the carryall at full throttle down a sheep path of a road that
was a shortcut—if he didn't cause a blowout taking
it. Several times Pamela had to get out and open and
close gates hung with weather-bleached signs. Once
they had warned, Posted, Keep Out, but the spring
dust storms had long ago eroded the message.

As he waited for her to close the last gate between
them and the collection of deserted hogans that made
up Mexican Springs, formerly called by the Navajo
name of Nakaibito, he had to ask himself why he was
trying to keep the Richardson guy from taking the
kid. After all, he was the boy's father. And since
Danny apparently hated Joe with a passion equal in
intensity to the passion Joe felt for Jaclyn, why
shouldn't he let Todd take Danny?

Because there's such a thing as ethics, even though
I was a fool to hope that things could ever have
worked out between two people from different
worlds.

When he spotted the two unoccupied cars at Mexican Springs ten minutes later, at first he felt relief.
He'd found them. Then his blood froze. Was Richardson deranged enough to kill Jaclyn and Danny?
He scanned the deserted hogans, then returned his
gaze to the two cars parked side by side. Jaclyn
would have taken the only path, the one that ran up
the face of the escarpment.

Danny was with her. His slightly pigeon-toed footprints were etched less deeply in the dust. Joe began to sprint along the narrow path, with Pamela following close behind. About a quarter of a mile along the trail, he came across Jaclyn's discarded alligator heels. Memories of another time, the same abandoned shoes, jangled his nerve endings. She had been in danger then, too. He quickened his pace. Behind him, he could hear Pamela drawing deep, rasping breaths. But she didn't complain or ask him to slow down.

In the dirt before him, he saw not only Richardson's prints, but Jaclyn's—their impression slightly deeper than they had been earlier. So, she was carrying Danny now. Up ahead, he heard shouting. The shortest way up the escarpment from here was a saddleback ridge. Motioning Pamela to go on along the trail, he started to climb the ridge, careful not to make any noise by dislodging stones.

Clearly now, he heard Jaclyn scream, "Run, Danny!"

His own breath labored, Joe scrambled down into a red sandstone defile and ran along the rock-walled passage. The passage opened onto a brush-rimmed clearing—and a view of Jaclyn struggling with a man. That split-second view of her assured him that she was all right, at least so far. Tears had made tracks down her dusty face, but she seemed unharmed.

In less than an instant he assessed the man. He fit
Jaclyn's description of her ex-husband: sandy hair,
suitably untidy; a suntanned face that reflected self-
esteem; an expensive but casual white jacket; and
creased jeans molding a body honed by hours at spas
and workout clubs.

In the following second he had Richardson by the
shoulder, spinning him around. Joe wanted to kill
the man for so much as touching Jaclyn. With his
solid fist he clipped Richardson under the chin,
driving the man's head up and back. His other fist
thudded into the soft triangle just below Richardson's ribcage. With a hissing gasp, the other man
stumbled back, his lungs sucking in air.

In that moment, as Todd gathered strength to
launch a retaliatory attack at Joe, Pamela came hur-
tling up the path into the clearing. "Get Jaclyn and
the kid," Joe shouted at her. "Get them out of
here!"

Pamela latched onto Jaclyn's arm, but Jaclyn re-
sisted the woman's tugging hands. "Joe!" Jaclyn
yelled. "I won't go. I'm—"

"Get out!" he repeated, his tone a command.

She cast him a frantic look, but obeyed, giving in
to Pamela's urgings.

Joe turned his own attention back to Richardson.
The other man made a diving lunge, and Joe went
sprawling. He grappled with Richardson, rolling
about on the rocky ground. At one point he caught

a fleeting glimpse of Danny, who was watching from the shadows of a clump of piñon. A jarring blow on the shoulder refocused Joe's attention on subduing the boy's enraged father. At last Joe gained the upper hand and came up straddling Richardson.

However handsome the man might be normally, the fury on his face now distorted his looks. His teeth gritted. "You son of a—"

"You're under arrest, Richardson. For attempting—"

In that same instant the *Yeibachai*, the gods of the supernatural, the gods of death, intervened. Joe spotted the rattler out of the corner of his eye, but it was too late. Like lightning, the snake, which had been coiled beneath the shallow ledge of a projecting rock, struck. The diamondback's fangs sank into the exposed flesh of Joe's forearm, just below his rolled sleeve; then the snake recoiled far back into the cavelike recesses beneath the ledge, out of striking range, but still rattling.

In a fraction of a second Joe's mind gauged his pain and flashed a warning: any further exertion would only speed the lethal venom's path through the body.

He tried to maintain his hold on Richardson, but in only seconds his pulse was thudding erratically against his eardrums. The bitten area had already swelled and turned purple. His body was weakening quickly. The pain crescendoed, and in a matter of moments was unbearably intense.

Richardson seized the advantage and rolled loose, then fled the clearing. For several seconds Joe lay stunned, attempting to apply logic to his thought processes. Even under the best of circumstances he would have had only a couple of hours to get help. But he hadn't been bitten under the best of circumstances. Not with his body pumping blood like a run-amok pump. Worse, the nearest poison control clinic with snake antivenin was in Gallup. From his perspective, a hell of a long way to go.

He managed to lever himself up onto one elbow, but he didn't have the strength to haul his heavy body erect. Searing pain electrified him. When he tried to yell for help, his voice was a mere rattle in the back of his throat. Who would have heard him, anyway? Pamela and Jaclyn and Danny were probably far down the escarpment by now—contending with a determined-to-have-his-way Richardson.

Even as Joe's brain cells began to shut down one by one, he blurrily saw the kid approach him. The dead-blue eyes stared down at him. Well, Joe thought in the still-functioning reaches of his mind, if that doesn't beat all. The kid gets his wish. Me out of the picture completely.

Chapter Eleven

Joe lay on the examination table in Gallup's Indian Hospital emergency ward while the doctor on call administered a dose of antivenin. The snake bite hurt like hell, and Joe tried concentrating on Jaclyn's lovely face, beside those of the nurse and intern at his side: the new-cream whiteness of her neck; the dark snare of her curls; the jewellike clarity of her erotic eyes.

It had been Jaclyn and Pamela, summoned by Danny, who between them had hauled him down the cliff. It had been an hour of pure agony. The injection the doctor had just given him hadn't been that pleasant, either, though it was a lot less painful than the rabies vaccine he'd had some years ago.

A white-capped nurse stuck her head in the room and asked Jaclyn, "Are you Mrs. Richardson?"

Jaclyn nodded. "Yes."

"Telephone. Long distance. You can take the call at the desk just outside. Line three."

Having administered the antivenin, the young intern was preparing to give Joe a follow-up tetanus injection. "Lucky the boy had the sense to take off your belt and band your arm with it," he said, holding up the hypodermic needle to see if any bubbles were stuck in the top of the syringe. He squirted an air bubble out and stuck the needle into the muscle of Joe's upper arm. "Otherwise you would have needed surgery, maybe even lost the arm."

What a kid. Joe's gaze sought out Jaclyn, who had reentered the room. "Where is Danny?"

Shadows of strain pooled beneath her eyes as she watched him with a love that should have made everything else in the world right, though it never would. "In the waiting room, with Pamela."

The intern interrupted to give Joe orders about resting over the next twenty-four hours, while the nurse dabbed the needle puncture with an alcohol-soaked cotton ball.

After they left, Jaclyn moved to his side. She took his hand between her smaller ones and held it against her cheek. Her skin felt like warm velvet. "I was so frightened, Joe. I thought I would lose you." She turned her cheek slightly, her lips seeking his fingertips to press feverish kisses on each one.

"What about Richardson?" He tried to control the rage in his voice. "Did he hurt you?"

She shook her head, her dark hair swaying against her shoulders. "No. He tried to make me get in his car with him, but..." She paused, then gave him her marvelous smile. "He was pretty winded from wrestling with you, and Pamela and I were giving him a hard time. She was pounding on his back with her fists, and I was kicking his shins—anyway, he gave up and took off. That's when Danny showed up and told us you were hurt."

"Danny... is he all right?" The boy's about-face attitude regarding him puzzled him.

Her smile sobered. "Oh, Joe, I thought I had lost Danny, too. I had thought he already escaped when Todd caught up with me there on the ridge. But he'd stayed behind to protect me."

"And me, it seems," he said wryly. "What made him do it? I'd have sworn he liked me about as much as a trip to the dentist."

She chuckled. "Well, about fifteen minutes ago, when he learned you were going to have to receive one of those nasty shots, as he put it, he confessed that he thought you were a pretty cool guy—especially when he saw you fight Todd on my behalf."

Her husband's name reminded Joe that there was still a job to do, and, without thinking, he tried to prop himself up on his arm. Closing his eyes, he groaned at the pain that shot through him. "Get Hofstetler. He's the deputy county sheriff."

Gently, tenderly, she pressed her hands against his chest, making him lie down again. "I know. While I was giving the admitting clerk information, Pamela called the sheriff's office to alert him about Todd. Hofstetler chased Todd for about twenty miles before he finally pulled him over and arrested him. Apparently Todd has a sensitive streak in him somewhere that even he can't snuff out. He confessed to having left you in the mountains, snake bitten."

He looked up to find her eyes caressing his face. "He could face a tidy bundle of charges: speeding, leaving the scene of an accident, attempt to do bodily harm, resisting arrest." He caught her wrist, shakily rubbing his thumb against her pulse and feeling it race at his touch. "I plan to personally see to it that he never touches you again." He felt ridiculous, making such a statement when he couldn't keep his own hands off her.

The shadow left her eyes. "You won't have to worry about that. For one thing, I think Todd finally realizes that I'll never give Danny up and I'll never go back to him. For another, the telephone call I took—that was his father. He had just finished talking with the family lawyer. It seems that both family and legal pressures are going to be put on Todd to accept the divorce and go his own way."

She leaned over and brushed his lips with hers. A sweet ache spread through him, diluting the pain. "You're better than any medicine," he told her. Her hands were still splayed atop his chest. In those loving hands he might find peace, he thought.

"Joe, I'm through running. I can help Old Martha and the others on the reservation. And Danny can have a normal childhood. I've come to realize, almost too late, that reservation life, for all its hardships, is uncomplicated, pure and rich in ways other than worldly goods. Joe, I love you so much. Don't look at me like that!"

It was the hardest thing he'd ever had to do. He cupped her face in both hands and said, "It won't work, Jaclyn. Don't you see that you're still running, still hiding, even here?"

"No," she cried. "No, don't you see that all the time I was running here, running to you?"

"What about Danny? He would be in a minority, the way you once were. And what about you? Soon you would began to hate reservation life, and then you would hate me. I couldn't stand that. For Danny's sake—and yours—you have to return to your own world."

He saw her flinch, but he kept his features firm, emotionless, though he was selfishly tempted to relent. As he watched her mutely suffering, it was as if he himself were standing with a rifle pointed at his chest.

At that moment the nurse entered with a prescription. While she explained to him about a follow-up visit, Jaclyn, her face pallid with ragged desperation, silently left the room.

The sacred wind of your spirit I breathe, he thought.

But the sacred wind was gone.

Jaclyn was striving to remake a life for herself and Danny in Vancouver. Joe had been right. Danny didn't belong on a reservation. Her son was settling nicely into the routine of second grade. Since Todd had rarely been home, Danny didn't miss his absence. As for Joe Watchman, BIA Indian detective, her son never mentioned him, and neither did she.

She had sold the house in Albuquerque, and with the settlement she had received from the divorce and the child support Todd was paying, she had enough money that she wouldn't have to work for some time to come. She could stay home with Danny. Still, time pressed heavily against her chest, making the mere act of breathing almost an effort.

The ranch-style house she had bought just outside Vancouver was nestled among thickly needled firs and spruce, and lovely, white-blossomed madroña that cast their reflections on the branch of the mighty Columbia River that flowed past the house. She had bought Danny a fishing rod, and every afternoon, after the school bus dropped him off, he would grab the rod and head for the river.

But for her, most days were dreary, with gray clouds hanging low over the river valley. Always the heavy mist . . . always the sodden earth.

On days like today, when the sky was dark, she would simply lie in the wicker chaise longue on the glassed-in back porch and stare out at the rushing river. Oh, she had things she could do: go to a bridge party, grocery shop, attend a PTA meeting.

But nothing could ease the ache inside her. She didn't know what to do with the pain of her loneliness. The pain of living without Joe was there all the time, gnawing at her. Day and night had become the same to her, equally without meaning.

Only the activity of observing nature gave her some surcease: watching a madroña move in the breeze off the river; observing a flock of snow geese winging south in their straggling vee formation.

Sadly she thought that, just as the geese made the southward trek every autumn and the salmon swam up the Columbia River to spawn every spring, she, too, inevitably obeyed nature's unseen signals, yearning for the desert when the rains poured. Yearning, though she strove not to, for Joe Watchman.

Even if she closed her eyes, she couldn't shut out the taste of his lips, or the feel of his hair against her flesh. She lived with a horrible sense of loss, as though parts of herself had been torn away. Phantom pain, amputees called it.

She missed him terribly... missed him... missed him all the time.

The air turned suddenly cool, and in the next moment the clouds wept copiously for her. Thunder rattled the window panes with sepulchral shock. Wind thrashed the trees. Lightning lit the clouds in eerie flashes that beat back the darkness.

One flash of lightning illuminated a solitary figure striding from beneath the sheltering trees. Mist haloed him. She rose from the chaise longue and pressed her hands flat against the glass. She murmured something. A prayer. Whispered hope. What if it wasn't Joe? Her pulse throbbed against her temples like the thunderclap that vibrated the windows, sending tremors through her hands, and from there all through her body.

Shakily, she took one step, then another. Then she was outside, running through the deluge and shouting his name. "Joe! Joe!"

Her hair clung to her cheeks, and her saturated clothes were plastered to her shivering skin. She ran straight into his arms. With the heavens opening around them, they kissed thirstily. Rain pelted their faces, soaked their lashes, seeped into their mouths. As if she were blind, her hands made reassuring movements over his sensual, strong-boned body: his iron shoulders, his thick neck, his high cheekbones and knife-blade nose. His large hands cupped her hips, pressing her against him as if to absorb her. They kissed and kissed, and she gasped beneath his clever lips and pleasure-giving hands.

Lightning scissored the dark sky and exploded in the forest. At the crackling crash, they lifted their heads and laughed for pure joy as the rain washed away their hurt and heartache. Still holding her tightly, as though afraid she would evaporate like the mist, he said, "I love you and I need you." From beneath water-spiked lashes, his eyes roamed lovingly over her rain-glistening features. "You are my Rainbow Maiden, Jaclyn, my guardian spirit. Your love will encompass me wherever I go."

"Oh, Joe, I love you. I love you." She discovered that it wasn't just raindrops coursing down her cheeks. She was weeping.

He placed his knuckles under her chin and tilted it. "Jaclyn, I have to tell you that I realized I was running, too. Night after night, I sat outside and watched the stars make their journey across the skies, and I knew that I would never find peace until I stopped running, until I made my peace with your world, until you became mine."

Her smile was as bright as the sudden shaft of sunlight through the clouds. "Welcome to my world, Joe, darling," she whispered.

* * *

The storm had moved out of the river valley. Late afternoon sunlight filtered through the glassed-in porch to glitter like fairy gold over Jaclyn. From the wicker chaise longue, she watched the river rushing to the sea and the geese honking southward. And she watched her son, fishing pole slanted across one shoulder, walking companionably alongside Joe toward the river. Danny's free hand was waving in vivid description of whatever he was telling Joe. No doubt about the eight-pounder that got away.

Going against a nightmare of experience, Joe was sacrificing his way of life to be with her and Danny in the white man's world. But wasn't that what love was about? Compromises and sacrifices for the sake of something more worthy?

Joe's unconditional love for her was still startling in its wonder. Before Danny came home from school, she and Joe had made an agreement that if he began to feel locked into step by his old FBI job, they would return to the reservation at least for part of the time, and work out some other solution for the rest of the year. Together, they could battle their separate fears and old nightmares.

She must have dozed off, because when she opened her eyes Joe was leaning over her, his hands braced beside her. She turned her face to catch his gentle, hot, passionate kiss. He nuzzled her temple, where wisps of hair caught the sun. "I didn't realize that I could ever know so much happiness," he said.

She felt that way, too. She was so happy that she found it hard to swallow. She framed his face in her hands, tenderness washing through her. "Next time, my love, we run away together."

* * * * *

Silhouette Romance

This month, some of your all-time favorites have returned to their "alma mater." Next month, some of the continuing stars of the Silhouette Romance line join in the celebration. Don't miss it—come home to Romance.

"Homecoming Celebration"

COMING NEXT MONTH

#532 WOMAN HATER—Diana Palmer
To Nicky White, rugged Montana rancher Winthrop Christopher was irresistible. But he wasn't moved by her charms. Could Nicky convince a confirmed woman hater to love again?

#533 MYSTERY LOVER—Annette Broadrick
Some men send flowers, some send cards, but Chad sent his thoughts—by telepathy. Jennifer loved him, but would she ever see her mystery lover face to face?

#534 THE WINTER HEART—Victoria Glenn
Actress Amanda Ryan was dedicated to her work—and to raising her sister's orphaned child. Then she met unfeeling Brad Winter—her niece's uncle. Could Amanda bring warmth to Brad's winter heart?

#535 GENTLE PERSUASION—Rita Rainville
Even though Kaylie West was the only witness to a robbery, she wasn't worried. But ex-Green Beret Adam Masters knew he had to keep her safe—even if he spent the rest of their lives doing it....

#536 OUTBACK NIGHTS—Emilie Richards
Model Rusty Ames was tired of the rat race; Australia was about as far from New York as she could get. But would a trip into the outback with devilish Aussie Daniel Marlin change her life forever?

#537 FAR FROM OVER—Brittany Young
When dignified lawyer Pierce Westcott met impulsive private eye Samantha English, he had no idea what he was in for. She had a knack for trouble, not at all the kind of woman he'd want for a wife—or was she?

ATTRACTIVE, SPACE SAVING BOOK RACK

Display your most prized novels on this handsome and sturdy book rack. The hand-rubbed walnut finish will blend into your library decor with quiet elegance, providing a practical organizer for your favorite hard-or-soft-covered books.

Only $9.95

Approximately 16" x 8" when assembled

Assembles in seconds!

To order, rush your name, address and zip code, along with a check or money order for $10.70* ($9.95 plus 75¢ postage and handling) payable to *Silhouette Books.*

Silhouette Books
Book Rack Offer
901 Fuhrmann Blvd.
P.O. Box 1396
Buffalo, NY 14269-1396

Offer not available in Canada.

BKR-2A

*New York and Iowa residents add appropriate sales tax.

Silhouette Intimate Moments

Starting in October...

SHADOWS ON THE NILE

by

Heather Graham Pozzessere

A romantic short story in six installments from best-selling author Heather Graham Pozzessere.

The first chapter of this intriguing romance will appear in all Silhouette titles published in October. The remaining five chapters will appear, one per month, in Silhouette Intimate Moments' titles for November through March '88.

Don't miss *"Shadows on the Nile"*—a special treat, coming to you in October. Only from Silhouette Books.

Be There!

IMSS-1